HOOKED ON YOU

THE BOOK AT THE BAR SERIES
BOOK 2

KIRAHVI BELLO

Copyright © 2024 by Kirahvi Bello

All rights reserved.

No part of this publication may be reproduced, distributed, or transmitted in any form or by any means, including photocopying, recording, or other electronic or mechanical methods, without the prior written permission of the publisher, except as permitted by U.S. copyright law. For permission requests, contact Kirahvi.reads@gmail.com.

The story, all names, characters, and incidents portrayed in this production are fictitious. No identification with actual persons (living or deceased), places, buildings, and products is intended or should be inferred.

Book Cover by Che'Naomi Durant (OG)

Illustrations by Canva

1st edition 2024

 Created with Vellum

OTHER TITLES BY KIRAHVI BELLO

The Book at the Bar

PLAYLIST

Apple Music Playlist

Spotify Playlist

YouTube Playlist

Bare Wit Me by Teyana Taylor
Little Death by The Beths
Entropy by Beach Bunny
Sip Into Something Soft by Hiatus Kaiyote
24 Hours by Young Deji
Tonight by Summer Walker
Anything by SWV
Outta My Mind by Chlothegod
Wake Up in the Sky by Gucci Mane, Bruno Mars & Kodak Black
Love Jones by Leon Thomas & Ty Dolla $ign
Vibes Don't Lie by Leon Thomas
Cognac Queen by Megan Thee Stallion
Sexyy Please by Sexyy Red
Rodeo by City Girls
Drop Top by Anycia
Blue Flame Ballet by Big K.R.I.T
In the Air by Kari Faux & Curren$y
How's My Driving? by PHABO
Never Lose Me by Flo Milli
Tell My by Joey Bada$$ & Chloe
Return 2 Sender by Dyl & Yaj
Spin by Megan Thee Stallion ft. Victoria Monet
SpottieOttieDopaliscious by Outkast

Pretty Mama! By AYLO ft. myquale
Big Bag by Tyler, The Creator
Sleigh Ride by TLC
Winter Paradise by Destiny's Child
The Christmas Song by Nat "King" Cole
Wrap Me Up by Jhene Aiko
Stick by Dreamville, JID & J. Cole ft. Kenny Mason &
Sheck Wes
SPAGHETTII by Beyonce, Linda Martell & Shaboozy
BLACKBIIRD by Beyonce, Tanner Adell, Brittney Spencer
So I Don't Feel Useless by Dianna Lopez
Self Care by Savannah Cristina
Could Be by Charity Green
Copper Cove by Latto ft. Hunxho
Frank by Alina Baraz
Please Don't Stay by Marvin Gaye
YES IT IS by Leon Thomas
So Fine by Mint Condition
Softest Place On Earth by Xscape
Bae Goals by Megan Thee Stallion
Rose by Chloe
1+1 by Beyonce
As by Stevie Wonder
II HANDS II HEAVEN by Beyonce
Nasty by Tinashe
LET HER COOK by GloRilla

BEFORE YOU READ

This book features...
* Explicit sexual scenes
* Drug use
* PTSD
* Depression
* Gun violence.

Please take care of yourself while reading.

AUTHORS NOTE

This book can be read as a stand alone. But, there are spoilers, circumstances and conversations that come from the first book in the Book at the Bar series.

This book dives into the life of Casey, Calvin's younger sister.

Enjoy!

DEDICATION

I dedicate this book to the people who have a dream that feels
deferred.

This is for to the lovers, the dreamers and the people that just
want to do their own thing away from their family.

PRELUDE

Casey chuckled into Denver's cabin as she had the past two nights. She needed this retreat to truly relax with some weed and good dick. Being tangled up in his bronze skin and hazel green eyes had been refreshing. She truly enjoyed sleeping with her fingers in his short, loose browns curls.

After another early morning round, they went to the main cabin for a catered brunch. It was Sunday morning, her last day at this retreat and she planned on indulging in more of Denver, her favorite retreat fuck buddy. Maybe she could squeeze in a sleigh ride or another trip to the gift shop for custom rolling papers. As they fixed their to-go plates, he gave her the eye that she was familiar with. *Love.* She didn't care, though. She was just here for a good time.

They grabbed their plates and headed back to his cabin. Denver just relocated to Denver, Colorado for a new job. So that's what she decided to call him. She also *completely* forgot his real name after they talked for three hours. His green eyes, freckled tan skin and muscular body kept her occupied on her solo vacation. He even massaged her feet while they were in the hot tub that morning, which led to her feet doing other things to him to say thank you. He loved that shit, too.

But from the looks of his living room as they walked in, this night was not going the way she planned. Red and white rose petals covered the floor from the door all the way to the bed in the corner. White candles in elaborate candelabras were lit casting a sexy and romantic glow throughout the room, and silver and red balloons hung in heart shaped bunches floating towards ceiling.

It was the largest display of love she had ever seen outside of a social media post from a random couple after he cheated on her three times and she stayed.

"Oh my God." Was all the swam out of her throat?

"Surprise! Do you like it? I've had such an amazing weekend with you, that I never want it to end. I know it sounds crazy, but when you meet someone you see a future with , you have to take the chance. I can't risk not having you in my life." There was a dazzle in his deep, hopeful eyes as he opened his arms to her.

Oh no, she said to herself. Why did she feel like he was about to ask her *least* favorite question?

"I want to be your man. Can we make us official?" He asked as his emerald eyes gleamed at her, waiting for her to move from her hometown of Atlanta and 'kickstart' her new life in Colorado and say yes.

"Uh Denver, this is- this is like the third day we've known each other. Do you think I'm crazy? How would it even work? You live in Colorado and I'm in Georgia! This is way too much. This wasn't supposed to be anything serious. I can't do this."

She slowly backed out of the door, feeling for the doorknob behind her back. His face read nothing but shock as she cringed and closed it. *Run bitch just in case he's behind you with a bow and arrow.* Once the door was closed, she quickly turned around and ran like a track star, as much as the snow would let her. She wasn't supposed to leave until two that next afternoon, but she grabbed her bags and booked the first Uber to the airport.

After her failed attempted of booking another flight, she waited seven hours, hoping and praying he didn't follow her. There were cameras and security at the airport. Someone would have a record of where she was, so it would be better to be waiting for a flight instead of in a cabin at a cannabis retreat where the man she was avoiding knew she slept there. The same retreat where the man that has only known her a few days wanted to cuff her.

Be official? With a stranger? No thanks. That was not what she signed up for. He was moving way too fast. She knew her pussy was good, but damn not 'make a man go crazy for her' kind of good. She just wanted to smoke and fuck with the mountains as a backdrop. Not a love story.

As she waited for her flight, she blocked Denver on everything. On the plane back to Atlanta, she wanted to forget everything. She *needed* to forget everything. She texted the next dick to pick her up from the airport, fuck her to sleep. Then leave.

CHAPTER 1
A YEAR LATER

WHEN CASEY MADE it to her gate at the airport, she noticed a restaurant close by. She looked at her watch, "I have two hours to kill. I could get a mimosa."

She could feel the eyes of other people watching her and she strutted with her pink carry on towards the restaurant. She was wearing black leggings, stilettos and a comfy pink pullover.

Sitting down at an empty table, a waitress approached her immediately. "What can I get you miss?" The middle aged woman said with a smile.

"I'll have two mimosas, scrambled eggs, toast and jelly."

She technically missed breakfast but needed to have something on her stomach. She took pride in her body and everything she consumed, which meant salads and anything healthy. She finally lost some weight and she was determined to keep it off. That didn't mean she never ate anything fried, but she would work it out on the pole. She wasn't plus size or even considered petite; it was more of that awkward place in between when you're blessed with wide hips but not height to balance it out.

"Comin' right up," the waitress said with a nod and walked away.

Casey was in charge of training the performers (*dancers, strippers, whatever*) for Grant Enterprises, her family's clubs, across the country. Not only did she standardize the way they trained at every location, but she also created a mentorship program for new performers to partner with someone more experienced for emotional support and encouragement. The program was already reducing the turnover of performers, which meant Coraline was saving money, which made Coraline and her happy. Her big sister CEO was happiest when she was making money and Casey was happy to travel on the company dime.

Casey had a bachelor's degree in dance and the same concepts could be used on the pole. Ballet for example, is all about the straight lines, pointing your toes and being balanced and graceful. The same can be said for pole dancing. Casey's pole studio should be opening in April and she couldn't wait to start classes.

After that, she was on her own.

If she launched in April, she was sure to pay the rent ahead on the space from revenue. She definitely didn't want the extra bill of it now. Her mom thankfully paid for the space a year in advance.

As Casey was admiring her favorite pole influencer on Instagram, a shadow appeared next to her. She slowly dug in her clutch for her pepper spray, *no guns in the airport.* Her heels were pointy enough to penetrate skin so that was another option. She curled her toes in preparation, then noticed the men's shoes. Cowboy boots?

She slowly looked up. The dark blue denim and an ironed grey t shirt. *That chest looks familiar.* It was Mr. Eye Candy Denver himself. He had a dashing smile and strong jaw line. As soon as his green hazel eyes made contact with hers, she froze. His face still had the same freckles as his eyes crinkled from his smile. His skin was a little darker, but still tan.

He looked more fit than the last year. His shoulders were tighter and she could see his pecks pushing through his dry fit shirt. She immediately became jealous if TSA had to pat him down. She hadn't seen him since she went to the retreat last year in Colorado.

He opened his arms for a hug. "It's good to see you Casey." His cozy voice said above her.

It snapped her back into reality. She slowly pushed her chair back and stood up, wrapping her arms around his neck. *Mmm his sweet musky cologne.* Her body unintentionally leaned into him more as his big hands cradled her lower back, his thumb gently brushing across her spine. She had to stop herself from biting his shoulder. She couldn't stop her nipples from tightening.

"Hi," she hummed against his ear. "It's good to see you too." Her hands brushed from his square shoulders, down his defined arms. He definitely was spending more time in the gym. She could feel it, and wanted to feel it more.

"May I join you?" he asked, piercing her eyes and giving her his best charming smile.

Casey's lips twisted as she looked him in the eye, studying his eyes. She knew if they fucked again, he would get obsessed. *Maybe he never stopped.* "Sure, we have to catch up. A lot has happened since last year."

As they both sat down, the mimosas and the breakfast order came. "Oh were you expecting someone?" He asked admiring the second glass.

"No I just thought I'd get ahead since they weren't bottom-less. But you can have it."

He nodded and grabbed the glass. "Thank you love." It looked tiny in his large hands. Casey tried not to think about the first time his hands were on her. At the retreat, she winked at him from the across the room and he joined her at the bar that overlooked the beautiful mountains. He kept buying her infused drinks, she kept rolling blunts and one thing led to another. She woke up in his room with 4 empty room service trays and his warm arm around her body. It was a cozy feeling that she enjoyed, so she decided to keep fucking him. Then after the roses, candles and ballons, she ran.

"What brought you to Houston?" He asked taking a sip.

She took a deep breath. She remembered how he looked on one knee. The hope vanishing from his eyes as she walked out of his door. "I'm just doing a tour of our businesses with no notices to see how they're really doing. Coraline is CEO now and doesn't want to open any new locations for awhile. I don't like staying in one place for too long, so I asked if I could check in on Houston. Now I'm headed back home to Atlanta." She smiled wider, thinking of the familiar skyline on 85. "What about you?"

"My job sent me to this conference. At first it was in Houston, but there's a second series happening in Atlanta. Since I did so good, they decided to send me to that one too." He eyed her up and down in a way that sent her body on fire.

She turned her head and fake coughed, avoiding his piercing eye contact. His looked immediately changed to concern as he grasped her hand.

"You okay, Casey?"

She patted her throat for show. "Mmhm mmhm. Atlanta you say? Where's your hotel?" She took another sip.

"It's in Midtown. I'll be there for a week."

A week. A whole week of Denver in the same city as Casey. There was no way she was going to resist him for that long. She already wanted to hug him again so she could rest her breast on his pecks. "Oh wow, a whole week? That must be a good conference."

"Yea." He looked away. "I was actually going to call you when I landed. If you didn't still have my number blocked."

Her eyes widened with raised eyebrows. "Whaaat?! Let me check."

She took out her phone and searched his contact. *Yep she knew he was still blocked.* Even though he sometimes crossed her mind since his ill-timed proposal, she hadn't unblocked him. She looked at her phone, then back to his eyes. A little fun won't hurt while he's in town, **unblocked**. "I just unblocked you. Sorry."

He shook his head. "No need to apologize. I came on pretty strong last time we were together so I couldn't blame you. Remember the cabin?"

Casey's entire body got hot as she took a bite of her toast and eggs. Her core throbbing from the memories. The server came and saved her. "Would you like to order sir?"

"No this is fine thank you." He smiled as he opened his wallet and gave her two 20 dollar bills. "Please keep the change." The waitress smiled and walked away.

Casey rolled her eyes. "I can pay my own way thanks."

Denver's fingers lightly brushed the top of the black table. "I know you can. But I don't know if this will be the last time I'll see you so I have to enjoy it."

Casey twisted her lips as she finished her mimosa. "Mmhm."

Denver folded his hands on the table, admiring Casey. She tried to ignore him, but lost. She thought he was fine from the first moment they made eye contact. As much as she tried to fight the force pulling them together, it never went well. She wanted to wrap her limbs around him, but not be committed.

She wanted to lick him like it was the last scoop of ice cream in her cone.

"Are you on the flight leaving in an hour or so?" he asked.

She nodded. "Yep, you?"

He nodded. "Yep. Where's your seat?"

"Economy. Coraline doesn't like to spend the first class ticket money like mom would. It's a shame really. Everything is 'bottom line' this and 'quote' that. She's so serious for no reason."

He rubbed his chin. "There's an open seat by me in first class. If you want to tolerate me for the two hour flight."

She scoffed. "So I disappear for over a year, and now you want to upgrade my seat to first class, with your own money. I know you don't want to let me out of your sight." Casey chuckled. "What would we even talk about Brian?"

He dramatically gasped and grabbed his chest. "Oh! You do remember my government name? Or did you cheat and look at my plane ticket? You've called me Denver ever since we met. It's a cute nickname, I've gotten used to it."

Casey rolled her eyes. She did glance at the plane ticket hanging out of his pocket though.

"How about you can think of it as a pre-thanksgiving gift then."

Casey turned to see the growing line of people at the gate. She always wiped her seat with a disinfectant wipe before sitting, but what if there was a crying baby? Maybe more time with Denver wouldn't be too bad. It had been a few months since she'd been in first class and the complimentary drinks were calling her name.

"Okay fine. But I'm only doing it for the drinks."

His smile grew, the hope showing in his eyes again.

Casey could resist his charms for two hours right?

CHAPTER 2

DENVER PICKED up her suitcase and stowed it away next to his in the overhead bin as she wiped down their seats and the window. "You know they clean the plane before you get on, princess." A nasty voice said behind her. Casey ignored him.

He clearly rose his voice, "Hey jackass, it would take two cans of Lysol to clean your mouth. You look like the type that has never worn a mask before."

The man grumbled and moved on to his seat.

Denver sat down next to Casey.

"I didn't know you had a little bark in your bite, I was just going to ignore the dick. They aren't about to kick me off this plane."

"I can't stay quiet when it comes to people I care about, sorry. I know our friend line is thin, but I won't tolerate disrespect. You are too important for that. Too important to me..."

The flight attendants went through the safety protocols and started getting the first round of drink orders while passing out warm towels.

"See this is what I missed, a nice towel while we take off," she whispered with a sigh.

He nodded, "So update me on your family? How's Calvin doing?"

She beamed; she could talk about her brother all day. "He's doing great actually. He's engaged to Gemini, even though he almost fucked it up. I would've beat his ass personally. But Gemini is really sweet, they are great together. She and I have started getting closer, too, so I like that. They even redid their place and it's super cute. She has brought out a softer side in him. It's gross, but adorable."

"That's good to hear! The pictures from the engagement party looked really good."

Casey's neck almost broke. "How did you know!? You *have* been spying on me!"

Denver's lips pressed together. "I plead the fifth."

She squinted her eyes at him. "All these months, you've just been watching me. Why didn't you slide in my DMs?"

"You blocked my number, enough was said. You obviously didn't like what happened at the cabin so I just gave you space."

The cabin again. Her heart dropped to her gut. The flight attendant placed their drinks and snacks down in front of them with a smile. "Thank you," Casey said with a sheepish smile, she swirled the mimosa as she stared into the flute.

Denver brushed her hand with his index finger. "Hey, I didn't mean to throw that in your face. I get it. We only knew each other three days and you walked into a rose covered room asking you to move states away from your family. Again, I'm sorry I came on so strong. I've been taking some serious time for myself and by myself, I don't want you to feel forced to talk to me."

She looked him in the eye. "Thank you for saying that. I apologize for ghosting you, I just, freaked out. I thought we were just having fun so it was a lot to process. I also don't see myself as the relationship or marrying type. Life is too fun to be tied down, right?" she chuckled. "Thanks for not showing up to my job to kill me."

He gasped. "I could never. What would the world be without Casey Grant? It would be filled with less fun and pink."

She rolled her eyes. "Don't get starry eyed now. I'm just here for the seat upgrade." She shoved his shoulder.

He chuckled. "I'll still enjoy it while I can. Want to listen to some music? We can share headphones?"

"I have my own thanks."

He smiled his dashing, charming smile at her. "But wouldn't it be cuter if we shared?"

She made a face and his eyes twinkled. *Fuck, why is his face so sit-able when he does that?* "Give me the headphone, at least I'll see what music you like but I doubt *I'll* like it."

Yes! He cheered to himself.

She held open her hand. He gave her a headphone and started intently scrolling his playlists. She pressed her lips together, trying to not think about how good he smelled. *Could they join the Mile High Club?*

Then a Taylor Swift song hit her ear. She slowly turned towards him, her pussy now dry. "So this is what you wanted to lead with Mr. DJ?"

He shrugged. "Taylor puts out good music. I may or may not be a Swiftie."

She roared with laughter. "We listen, and we don't judge. But I REFUSE to listen to her the whole flight."

He nodded. "The DJ is too cute to fire right?"

She eyed him with a smile, "Yea, too cute."

When the third mimosa came, the playlist was in full swing

with alternative bands Casey's never heard before. She asked about a few songs but didn't want to seem too interested in them. Although she was making mental notes. "I fuck with this music. I forgot how much I missed listening to actual bands."

"Exactly!" A wide smile spread across his face as he admired her. "Are you sure you want to listen to my music the whole way?"

She tried to ignore the light in his eyes as she crept her hand towards his.

"Your music is growing on me. Please send me the playlist." A half smile on her face. "Now I'll send you one of my playlists to listen to next."

His cheeks burned as he accepted the hand hold.

As they stepped off the plane, a flight attendant said, "Y'all look so cute together. Enjoy your time in Atlanta!" Casey didn't care about correcting her, especially since they were still holding hands.

That's weird, I don't want to let go.

CHAPTER 3

CASEY AND DENVER got out of the elevator. His hand was on her lower back as she unlocked the door to her condo.

She opened the door and her home was just as she left it, spotless. The condo complex also had a cleaning service, so she made sure to make an appointment before she came home, just in case. She was glad it was Friday night. She could glide into the weekend, then visit the studio first thing on Monday. Since Coraline had a new assistant, it made everyone's job easier. Casey adjusted her schedule to work four days a week at Grant Enterprises so she could have at least one day a week to prepare for the launch of the studio in the new year.

She kicked off her heels and exhaled as she held the door open for Denver. Her pink pole was on proud display in the corner of the living room, so she could still watch her wall-mounted TV. The kitchen was closest to the door with grey countertops, a deep sink and large fridge. Casey made a mental note to order groceries to be delivered.

Then there were windows the length of the condo with a balcony and patio furniture with an egg chair.

"Wow this is beautiful. It's very you. I like the pink and grey accents."

"Thank you, you know how much I enjoy pink." They chuckled. "Now it's time to wash this airport off of me."

Denver eyed her. Casey could tell he wanted to say something. She did invite him over and they had a lot of fun on the flight. He always made her feel fuzzy again and they picked up right where they left off.

Walking into her bedroom, she asked him, "Do you want to watch or join me in the shower?"

He blushed as he bit his bottom lip. "I'd love to do both."

Casey eyed him as she walked into to the bathroom. He was close behind her.

"Since I let you DJ on the flight, now it's my turn to play some music."

Denver placed his bag down on the bathroom floor. "Fair is fair." He said with a smile.

She turned on the shower and began playing music on her phone. Then "Only Fans "by Young Deji began playing throughout the entire bathroom.

"Oh, speakers in the bathroom walls? That's a nice touch. It'll drown out your screams tonight."

Casey turned with her mouth agape. "Who says I'll let you make me scream?" Her hair flying around her shoulders.

The corner of his mouth lifted. "I'm only doing what you tell me."

She slowly undressed in front of him. Her breasts bounced as she removed her top. Then she turned her back to him as she slipped down her pants and thong, shaking her ass as they fell. He rested his weight on the double vanity. Good. He didn't mind being teased.

She turned back around to face him again, showing what

he had missed. His eyes drank her in as she brushed her hands over her belly button, up her torso, lightly brushing her nipples to her neck, then wrapped her hair in a high bun. She made a good call getting a Brazilian wax the week before. Casey watched Denver's eyes as she opened her glass shower door and got in.

He continued to watch her lather her body in soap by the sink. He took his clothes off and grabbed his towel and body wash from his bag. He lightly knocked on the glass door.

"You may come in," she said teasingly.

The way he admired her body made her knees shake, but she couldn't let him see, though. He couldn't know the hold he had on her. He stood inches above her, his green hazel eyes never leaving hers. She didn't realize that as he started bathing, she froze. She needed to touch him.

"Do you mind if I wash your back?" She asked breathlessly.

"Oh of course not ma'am." He handed her the cloth and she slowly washed each line of muscle in his back. She reached and got behind his strong shoulders. Then his ass, so caramel, beautiful and tight. She squeezed his cheek and he looked over his shoulder. "Havin' fun."

"Most definitely."

He rinsed off his body, looking down at her wet gorgeous body. Casey took a step towards him, reached her hand behind his neck and kissed him.

He sighed into her mouth as they kissed deeper, the shower water and steam surrounding them. Denver squeezed her hips and turned so that the water hit his back. He bent down and whispered in her ear, "I'd hate for your hair to get wet baby." He kissed her jaw.

"Mmm such a good boy."

She brushed her nails from his neck, down his cut chest,

brushing past his nipples to his hard dick that was pressed against her stomach. She massaged his length as she watched his head lean back into the shower water. The water flowing down his hair and shoulders.

"Aww damn Casey," he whispered. His hands began working their way around her body until his hands met her erect nipples. He lifted her breast and brought it to his mouth.

Casey groaned as she lifted into his mouth more. "Baby baby, don't stop. I'm gonna come already, fuck." He lifted her knee with his other hand and began slowly playing with her clit. Her eyes rolled back as she panted, hoping her foot wouldn't slip.

"Mm stay still for me, I got you baby." Her knees almost buckled but he caught her. "I got you." As he slipped two fingers in, she groaned louder and came. Her lip quivering. His fingers twisting faster and faster. The waterfall going down his back and down her leg.

He straightened up and sucked his fingers as he glared at her. "You taste amazing, just like I remember."

Casey rinsed herself and turned off the water, grabbing her towel then handed Denver his. She watched him quickly dry off his body and run the towel through his now wet, dark brown hair. She was barely dry as she jumped on her vanity with her legs spread. The cool air covering her skin in goosebumps.

He wasted no time, positioning himself right in front of her, kissing and licking the water from her neck and the gap in her breast. Her breath hitched each time. Then he got on his knees and ate her like a juicy peach. She couldn't stop squirming and screaming as he sucked her clit. Her hand rested on his head, her nails in his hair. He finished with a loud slurp. "Mm you're the only woman I'll get on my knees for. You are so special."

She felt like melted ice cream.

He slowly stood up, looking down at her with fire in his eyes as he pressed his lips together. Casey brushed her hands across his chest as he pulled his waist into hers, his head teasing her soaked entrance. "I need it baby, give it to me." She groaned, looking up at him.

He gave her the dashing smile that made her forget her name, hooked his arms under her legs and easily slipped inside. The veins on his neck showed as he went deeper and deeper. "Damn Casey, your so fucking tight." He whispered as he slowly started stroking her.

"I know baby. I know you missed this pussy."

"And I'm about to show you how much."

A brown curl rested on his forehead as he pushed inside of her. She licked her top lip as she let him completely take over her. His face hardened as he breathed faster. Casey screamed as she dug her nails into his shoulder. The marks starting to show red.

"Fuck." They both groaned. They kissed each other crazily as he stroked her. She sucked her taste off his lips. The sounds of pounding bouncing off the tile walls just as loud as the music. Casey leaned her head against her bathroom mirror and Denver changed his angle inside of her. Her toes curled.

"I wish you could see how beautiful you look Casey. The faces you make, shit."

She bit her lip and looked him in the eye. "It's yours baby."

"All mine," he groaned. Her breast bouncing against his chest.

She slowly brought her hand to his neck and started chocking him. His wet curls rested on his forehead as he smiled. "Yes squeeze harder." As she tightened the grip on his neck, his face became soft. "I missed you so much Casey," he whispered.

"I missed you too Denver," rolled off of her lips before she could stop it.

He made eye contact with her and the energy in the room changed. He picked her up, and carried her into the bedroom, slowly placing her on top of the pillows. His big hands cradled the back of her neck. "What's my name? I want to hear you say it." He entered her again with more intent, rolling his hips as he admired her eyes. "You deserve this. I want to hear you say my name."

"Brian," she groaned against his lips as her hands brushed on his back. "Brian," she whispered again.

He kissed her slow, not missing a beat, lightly kissing her beautiful lips as he went deeper and deeper. She tightened around him as he rolled his neck.

"That's right. Let go for me baby," he instructed.

She melted into the sheets as she came again. He filled her so well, she didn't want him to stop. He kissed her cheek, her shoulders, her ears and jaw. Is this what love felt like? A shower of kisses in a room filled with passion. He playfully licked her nipples.

His eyes looked brighter in the dark. She lifted her head and kissed him as her nails brushed his scalp. "Ahh shit," his body began to quiver as he pulled out. He came on her leg just in time. He went to the bathroom and grabbed a wet cloth, cleaning himself and her leg. She was fighting sleep. She could still feel his strokes in her back.

"Get under the covers baby," Denver said.

She groaned and slowly got under her sheets. He chuckled as he joined her. She nudged him and he opened his arms. She smiled as he rubbed her back and kissed her temple.

∿

HER EYES slowly opened as the sunlight started to pour into the room. The beautiful man laid next to her asleep, his arm tucked under his head as his bare chest rose and fell. He snored quietly. She couldn't stop staring at him. She really liked him and it scared her because she didn't want him to leave. It was too powerful. She could feel the energy they brought.

But she still wanted to be single.

She slowly brushed her hand on his chest. He has toned up more since the last time they saw each other. His dark brown happy trail going to his belly button, the 6 pack lines at rest. She wanted more and she didn't know if she would have another chance after this weekend. He's only here for a week right? They might es well have some more fun.

Casey got under the cover and slowly put his dick in her mouth. As she eased and licked him, he groaned holding the back of her head. "Shit," he whispered above her. She started going faster and louder as he began to squirm, stroking her face. She slurped and licked his tip as she climbed on top of him. "Well good morning beautiful," he said groggily.

"Good morning," she said wiping her mouth as she lowered herself on him. He gasped and she groaned, slowly bouncing and squeezing her hips as she tossed her head back. His hands cradled her breast, pinching her. He worked his hips against her as his hands started to travel down her body. Then he lifted himself deeper into her. He didn't slow down as she began to scream. He smacked and squeezed her ass as he began to growl. She adjusted into a split, bringing her right foot next to his face.

"Damn," Denver whispered. "Still flexible I see."

Casey flipped her hair, flowing down her back. Her scarf discarded. "You know it baby. I'm riding the fuck out of you. I've missed your dick."

"He's missed you too baby. You're his one and only."

She tried to act like she didn't hear that last line, but it made her feel warm inside. She started twerking, "You want me to slow down? Do you want me to stop?"

He gasped coming back to life, "Fuck no! Please fuck me." She turned around and rode him in reverse.

He groaned that much louder. "Come here baby."

He grabbed her ass, lifted her up and brought it to his face. He dug in like it was his favorite meal. Casey tried to suck him again, but he smacked her ass.

"I didn't tell you to move, take this tongue." He pushed his face in deeper and took all of her into his mouth. When he started licking her cream, she couldn't stop her legs from shaking. He spread her cheeks even more, as she screamed into his chest.

"Can I put a thumb in?" He asked.

She was catching her breath. "Ye- yes," she heard him suck his thumb and slowly it slide it in. The change in pressure made her neck roll. She instantly came again. "Da-damn Denver."

He smacked her ass again. "Say my fucking name again."

"Briannnn," she groaned as she rode his thumb. His other hand began fingering her, her juices dripping on his face.

"You like that baby? You like how I take care of you?"

"Yes yes I do."

She could feel him smiling, "I know." He slowly sat up and laid her on her back, placing her feet on his shoulders. "I'm gonna keep giving you what you like baby, I promise."

Her body shuddered.

The morning sun was in the air by the time they unlocked from each other. Casey scrolled through her phone as he brushed his teeth and washed his face. Then he started digging in his luggage. "What are you doing?" she asked.

"Getting some briefs, is that okay with you?"

She frowned, "I guess but I need easy access to your package. Please and thank you."

"All you have to do is ask ma'am." He said in a heavy country accent. "Are you ready for some breakfast?"

"Yea the food in the fridge might be good, but check first." He walked into the kitchen and she listened as he started taking out pots and pans. She didn't want to be far from him. Not because she was falling for him or anything, she just enjoying looking at his physique move around her condo.

She rolled out her yoga mat in the living room and turned on her speaker. She began her morning routine as the sweet scent of coffee filled the place. She crossed her legs and prayed, then did 15 minutes of yoga. Her hips weren't about to lock up now. When she was on her hands and knees, she inhaled and exhaled changing from cat and cow. She glanced at Denver in the kitchen. He was watching her as her ass was in the air. "Enjoying the show?" She teased, it was then she realized that she was still naked.

He gave a devilish grin as he rinsed out a pot, "Anything you want for breakfast?"

"How about a breakfast sandwich? The croissants are in the bread box. Are they still good?"

Denver looked around the kitchen, found them and inspected. "Still good, what do you want on them?"

Casey smoothly transitioned to a downward dog, "Avocado, tomato, spinach and cheese with eggs on the side."

He opened the door to the fridge. "Wow your fridge is very aesthetic. How long does it take you to organize it in bins like this?"

She chuckled, lowering into a plank, "Not long. It's like ASMR to me at this point, fruits and veggies have to be washed anyways. I sometimes take pictures too just because I'm proud it's clean."

He nodded, pulling the ingredients out and turning on the stove.

When Casey finished, she walked up to the bar and watched him cook. He looked over at her, "How do you want your eggs?"

"A little runny but not too much." He nodded as he buttered the pan. "What kind of sandwich are you making for yourself?"

"Ham, cheese and bacon, nothing too serious."

Casey chuckled, "Okay double meat man."

They ate their sandwiches together and watched TV. She took the first bite and groaned. "This is so good, and you put some seasoning on it. Look at you!"

Denver rolled his eyes, "My mom used to be a pit master. Of course I use seasonings on my food."

She put her hands up, "Opps. I didn't mean to hurt feelings." She chuckled, "How is your mom doing? I forgot she owned that ranch." Casey didn't forget but wanted to know if she was doing well. Denver mentioned his parents briefly at the retreat.

He nodded and chewed. "She's doing good. It's starting to get cold there so her and the staff have been preparing the horses for winter. I'm planning on visiting her during Christmas."

"Aww that would be nice! Spend some time with the family horseback riding and stuff."

They sat quietly as they finished eating. After the food settled, Casey stretched for 10 minutes, then put on a pink sports bra and matching thong. She poured the pole grip on her hands and leapt onto her pole. She practiced her pulls up and spins while trying to mentally piece together routines for the studio launch. She lowered herself and grabbed her notebook from the bookshelf. She was determined to open her pole studio next year, which was technically in two months. She's already thought of a monthly package that with a monthly fee of $50, that would pay for three classes a week and $75 a month for all classes offered. But which classes?

She put the journal back down. She walked around the pole then went into a graceful chair spin. Then swung her leg so only her knee connected, her arms in a T. She smiled as she took a deep breath. Pole fitness was not easy, so once she mastered her moves and gained the upper body strength. She enjoyed it and enjoyed teaching people how to get there.

As she was hanging upside down, with an awestruck Denver watching her, his phone rang. "Oh shit I have to take this." He quickly stood up and ran into the bathroom.

She slowly descended into a somersault and turned down the music. Who could've called that was so important? A girlfriend maybe? Did he lie about taking time for himself?

I don't care, she whispered to herself. Well, maybe she did. She slowly walked toward the bathroom.

"I'm sorry I missed the networking breakfast this morning Mark, it wasn't on my calendar..... yea yea I'm in Atlanta my flight got in late last night.... Sure sure we can go over the skit changes again... no I can't today maybe Sunday?.... Tell Dave everything is done and will be perfect for Monday.... Alright see you tomorrow then."

Casey lightly tiptoed back into the living room and put her hand on the pole, just as Denver reappeared in the living room.

"Sorry about that, it was work. They don't believe in days off, but I'm getting one today." He widely smiled at her. "I just have to check into the hotel tomorrow to not lose the reservation. My colleague Mark is covering for me."

She tried to sound disinterested. "Oh okay cool, gives me more time to bother you," Casey said with a shrug as she gripped the pole, took a few steps and swung her leg in the air once again. But inside, she was glad that they had more time together.

Denver beamed. "Ooo you must be starting to like me. I fucked you pretty good huh?"

"Shut up!" Yes Casey was still feeling bubbly. Almost like she was floating.

He chuckled, "I'm yours all day."

Her eyebrow arched. "All day you say?"

He eyed her as he stood up, walking towards her slowly. "Mmhm, whatever you like."

She licked her lips, "Let me roll a blunt first. Not that I couldn't fuck the shit out of you right now. I just want to smoke first."

"That's fine by me, but you can't be smoked out by the champ."

Her face twisted, "The champ? Uh uh since when?"

"Since you gave me my nickname at the retreat," Denver chuckled. "You *thought* you could smoke my head off and got corrected. We were drinking the infused drinks and rolling on the complimentary papers remember? They tasted like strawberries."

She gasped, "Yea! They even had the cabin logos on them. That was a great marketing tactic. I never used flavored papers before."

"Me either, I could match you if you know a plug. I'd just have to go through it this week."

"I do actually and he delivers but you'd have to meet him in the parking garage."

Casey texted her plug, Greg, Denver's information so they could arrange it. While she was rolling two joints, he went downstairs. In the few minutes he wasn't in the condo, she missed his energy.

It was quiet.

It was nice being around a guy for more than a night. *Fuck I'm sprung this is gross.* It was only for a week. Next week was her sexy 26th birthday party at her favorite club and her studio launch in a few months. Things were lining up for her.

Shit! She hadn't told Denver about either of those plans. Oh well, he wouldn't come anyway.

CHAPTER 4

HE ALMOST DIDN'T RECOGNIZE his own name across
the screen. Casey came up with the Denver nickname the day
they met. The name stuck so good he forgot his government
name, Brian. Unless he made her call him that name. He
quickly texted his mom letting her know he wasn't kidnapped
or killed on his flight.

He never thought he would see Casey again, let alone
enjoy her too. He doesn't even want to mention trying to ask
her to be his girlfriend again. No. They had too much fun last
night. And this morning. The way she woke him up? He would
do the same to her *every* morning, without a second thought.
He had to mentally go into outer space to not come just from
the sight of her body in the shower.

She's lost weight, but she still had her full shape. She was fit, full and fine. But even if she wasn't, he still wouldn't mind eating it from the back. She had him under her thumb like a crumb. He wanted to give her all of him. But he had to pull back. He couldn't have a repeat incident. He really just wanted to do something nice for her. Something that she would remember him by. *Yea remembered me as the crazy guy who changed his mind on proposing at the last second and said girlfriend instead.*

Her place was exactly as he pictured it, spotless and pink. She even had a pink pole. He loved how it was on display. Something she can be proud of. He might just get one for himself. Maybe a video of him trying it out would make him more subscribers, leading to more money. Since he was 30 now, he needed to have a plan for retirement in his future. His body may not look this good forever. So stashing his *OnlyFans* money in a rainy day savings account and retirement fund were the best bets.

By day, he was an entertainer, hosting employee bonding and engagement activities at corporate retreats with Helping Human Helpers, the premier Human Resources company. By night, after the trivia nights and fun, he was on *OnlyFans*. His first post was two years ago and he had grown a steady following since. He'd gotten so popular that as long as he posted at least three or four times a week, he would be able to quit his day job. He enjoyed making people smile *and finish*. Women, and men, swooned at the sight of his bronze skin, hazel green eyes and chiseled upper body. Though, nothing was better than the sound of a room erupting into laughter, because of him.

They sat on the couch together. Casey was sitting criss cross applesauce next to him, her knee brushing against his leg. "Do you mind if I rub your feet?" he asked.

She made an approving face and wiggled her pink painted toes, extended her legs and sat them in his lap. "Of course not!"

He began rubbing smooth circles on her ankle and down her achilles heel. He couldn't stop himself from tickling the bottom of her feet, quickly working his way up to her waist.

Her laugh echoed and bounced off the walls. "Stop stop! I'm gonna pee if you don't stop!"

He quickly sat back up, "Sorry I couldn't resist."

She playfully kicked him and slowly placed her feet back on his legs. "Can I ask you a question and you promise to not judge me?"

His heart raced. What the fuck was she about to ask? *Did she find my page?* "Um sure." He said hesitantly, then started overthinking. *Does she want to date? Is this it? Are my dreams coming true?*

"What's your um, background? I never asked at the retreat. I just assumed you were white but you're kind of racially ambiguous. You were lighter back then." She looked away. "Brian is also a white ass name, so yea. I hope you don't mind me asking. I gave you the Denver nickname because that's a vibe you give off and you were moving to Denver at the time."

He put his hands back on her feet and she flinched. The question he's been answering his whole life. "Case, your good. I'm mixed."

Her eyebrows raised. "Oh, with what?"

"White and black. My mom is black and my dad is white. They've been married for over 30 years now. Also there are black men named Brian."

"Who?"

Denver thought for a moment. "Brian McKnight? That's someone."

Casey put her hand to her forehead. "That's literally the worse example you could've used." She laughed. "Can I see a picture of your parents? Since you stalked my socials you know what my family looks like."

He smiled as he lifted her feet to get to his pocket. He picked a selfie of them at his parents ranch house in Nashville. He was standing in between them in front of the garage. They were in matching t-shirts. His mom had a fresh silk press that went past her shoulders, her lips a deep red. Her gingerbread skin glowing, wrinkle free but with a beauty mark at her eyebrows and cheeks. His father had a fresh haircut with a fade and always got mistaken for Pierce Brosnan.

"You all look cute as hell. I love the grey in your parents' hair. They actually look really good together."

He smiled, "Thanks. They still live in Tennessee but I FaceTime them. Then when my dad starts showing my mom 'too much' love I tell them good night as fast as I can. They are still very much obsessed with each other. There is no trauma like hearing your parents fuck."

She laughed, "At least you see them in the same room. I haven't seen my parents in the same room in... years." She looked away and pulled her feet back to herself.

"What happened?" His voice was barely a whisper.

Casey's eyes glazed over. "Um. It's personal..."

He watched her wheels spin. *Tell me please tell me.*

"My parents were never really officially together. My mom wasn't a woman for... committed relationships. Me and none of my siblings have the same dad. My dad is in jail and has been for a long time."

It was quiet.

"I'm here for you." Denver rubbed his thumb on her elbow. She kept her hands folded in her lap. He couldn't help it but he wrapped her in a hug, bringing her onto his lap as his nose brushed the top of her head as he rubbed her back. She didn't cry, she just... shut down. But he would be there for her.

He would always be there for her.

CHAPTER 5

WHILE DENVER WAS asleep in the bedroom, Casey laid on the couch and decided to call Gemini on speaker. She answered on the second ring. "Hey Casey! How are you doing?"

"I'm good, what about you?"

"Good, another day. How's the studio coming along?"

She shrugged to herself, "Girl, I'm so scared. I'm stopping by there on Monday to clean." She gagged to herself. "And I hate cleaning. I've always paid someone else. But I gotta do it myself eventually so, here I go." Her voice dropped into disappointment and stress.

Gemini roared with laughter. "Girl what! Wow. You need to get it together soon 'cause nobody wants to be in a dirty place. It's your place, sooo you gotta clean it. Don't you clean your condo?"

"The building actually has a company that comes weekly, biweekly or monthly to clean and they charge it as a fee."

There was silence on the line. "Be so fucking for real right now."

"Your right Gem." She sighed. "I just don't want to ruin these cute ass hands."

"Wear some gloves then. You excited for your birthday though? It'll be my first time at a strip club so I'm excited. I already set aside what I'm wearing."

"Hell yea! I'm getting an entrance, red carpet, the princess gets what she wishes for."

"Ooopp okay then!"

Casey chuckled.

"I'm gonna be in your first class, anyway, no matter what. Teach me how to twerk on the pole." They laughter together. "Casey's Pole Studio will be an Atlanta staple in no time," Gemini said.

"You're opening a pole studio?" Denver's groggy deep voice asked entering the living room. "I didn't know." It made Casey jump.

"Fuck you scared me."

"Who is that?" Gemini asked.

"A friend of mine sis. I had you on speaker, my bad. Lemme call you later."

"Okay cool. Love you sis."

Casey gave Denver a worried look. "I love you too." And she hung up the call. He rolled his eyes and walked in the bedroom. Then pulled out his suitcase.

"You're opening a pole studio on your own?" She watched him try to force a smile, but it looked like it hurt him. "I'm proud of you."

"Yea I am. I don't have an official launch date yet. I'm aiming for April. I have the space paid for a year." He didn't need to know it was a gift from Mama.

He continued packing, "And the birthday party?" He tried to take the pain out of his voice.

"I forgot about that, too," she lied. "I want you there. It's at the Green Envy Gentleman's Club."

His eyebrows raised, "The biggest strip club in the city? It's one of the most popular clubs in the country, maybe even the world. How did you manage to reserve that? I've only heard of legends and famous people getting in. It's mentioned in like 30 songs."

Casey chuckled sitting on the foot of the bed. "My family owns it and has owned it since the 90s. I'll make sure your name is on the list. I'd actually like for you to ride with me."

Denver zipped up his suitcase. "Thanks for the invite."

He started wheeling it towards the door and Casey followed. Dusk was approaching and the condo was filled with the golden orange color of the setting sun. "I guess I'll see you later."

She gave him a half smile, missing him already but scared to say it out loud. "Yea, see you later." Then with a hard click, the door closed and he was gone.

Back to the quiet.

She laid across her couch and stretched as she grabbed the remote and her rolling tray.

She was fine.

She enjoyed the quiet. Tomorrow she was going by the studio to clean up and try to come up with an official opening day on the calendar. The launch has to be before June because she didn't want to be too busy around Gemini and Calvin's wedding. But if she launched after June, she may not make enough money to pay the rent next year.

Her mom only paid the rent for one year and not a cent longer. If she begged, she could get more. But she wanted to genuinely succeed. Coraline and Calvin thought everything was handed to her. They might be right, but she has a work ethic. She survived at a majority white middle and high school and won the best dressed superlative her senior year. Then graduated from an HBCU in four years. She could conquer anything she set her mind to.

In the back of her mind, she still wanted her MBA. She needed something to fall back on if everything fell apart. A black woman can keep getting degrees forever. The clubs would always make money but Casey always wanted more than that. The spotlight at Grant Enterprises only went so far.

She used to want to be a prima ballerina. The tutus, the leaps and turns… the way the air brushed her cheeks when she flew in the air. Even though pointe shoes murdered her feet, she went through the trouble of painting her shoes brown rather than leave them pink. After partnering with another girl in her college class, she never stopped painting them with old foundation. She deserved to have shoes that matched her skin tone. She even taught a kids' ballet class as an internship sophomore year of college. She worked at the local dance theater for a year and that inspired her to teach dancing. But when the internship ended, she couldn't find any other positions with a livable pay.

During her senior year at Spelman, she went to New York for a pole fitness class in Central Park. It was the most liberated she felt since putting on her painted pointe shoes for the first time. That's when she started practicing pole with the pointe shoes on. It was just a vertical bar, right? She figured it out and it quickly became her new quiet personal obsession. She ordered her pole from a black woman-owned business. It would be a dream if the owner came to teach a class. Once Casey got certified to become a pole instructor, virtually. She wanted to dive head first in the work.

That's why when the Dance Executive Trainer position was created at Grant Enterprises. An 'official' interview sealed her in the position. Unlike other clubs, Mama wanted her establishments to include girls doing choreography and switch it around. It kept the energy in the room bright and the money thrown. Other clubs had gotten lazy and we needed to keep going outside of the box. With Casey's fresh ideas and moves, it had shown success across the market. The other performers weren't on pointe, but it made a huge difference having duo and trio choreography for the main stage. But being in her empty condo just made her feel like she was being swallowed.

Denver kept that feeling away.

Loneliness, with a mix of dread when waking up in a cold bed. But it's still not worth sacrificing who she was for a man.

She turned on "*Something for Thee Hotties*" by Megan Thee Stallion and began to do some stretches. She eyed her notebook, just in case she had more pole combinations that came to mind. As she began tying the ribbon from the pointe shoes around her ankles, she was thankful to have the ability to order brown pointe shoes.

CHAPTER 6

CASEY PUSHED her key into the hole and turned. With a heavy push, she opened the door and walked into the pole studio. 10 poles had been installed while she was out of town. Calvin made sure they did their jobs and locked everything up. She tested each of them as she walked past, grabbing, twisting. The floor to ceiling length mirror was also installed last week and it helped everything feel more real. But the room still needed work. The floors and walls needed a good mop because of the thick layer of dust from the installation. Then a new fresh coat of paint. Now everything needed to be deep cleaned, again.

She walked to the large window overlooking the Beltline. There were people jogging, couples talking, holding hands, pushing strollers in bright biker shorts. She knew with this studio being in a heavy foot traffic area, it would lead to more people to teach. Who wouldn't want to learn to love or at least be curious to know how to spin on the pole? *I guess mom picked the place well.* After zoning out while people watching, she reminded herself she still needed curtains for protection.

Another thing added to the list. *It's always fucking something.*

She walked up to the wall length mirror and looked at her reflection, unsure if she was in her real studio. Casey still couldn't decide on the paint color, let alone when her opening day was. *Spring? Before June? After? March? April? Rent Rent Rent.* Tears started forming in her eyes, an overwhelming feeling consumed her. The weight. Was this a good idea? Maybe she should go back to lashes or nails?

No, she failed at those already.

She used the wrong glue and well... Mama had to pay the customer A LOT of money to not report Casey to the Better Business Bureau. *I'm a fuck up I know.*

A knock at the door made her jump up. Who knew she was here? She stood up and looked in the peep hole. Surprisingly, it was her brother, Calvin, with a mop bucket and a smile.

She sighed as she unlocked and opened the store front door.

"Hey Casey! I wanted to drop off some supplies you might need but didn't ask for."

She opened the door wider and let him in. "How did you know I was about to have a panic attack about cleaning and opening and just, everything?"

He gave her a sideways glance as he put down the bucket. "Casey, you begged mom to have a cleaning company clean your dorm room ALL four years that you were in college. We all know you don't like to clean. I also noticed you haven't really been talking about the studio with us so I wanted to see how you were doing with it."

She pressed her lips in a thin line and crossed her arms. "Mom said it would stay between us. I had disgusting roommates."

Calvin chuckled placing the supplies down. "Coraline told

me. You know no cent is spent that she doesn't know about. Let me get the rest of the stuff from the car."

Casey groaned. She always hated cleaning. It was dirty and could ruin her nails and hands. *I'm just a girl.... why do I have to clean.* When Calvin came back with wipes, cloths, gloves and cleaning solution, she groaned even louder. "Can't I negotiate? You clean, I watch, and treat you to lunch?"

Calvin's face flattened. "Ha. Hard pass. You have to learn how to do this sis. What if a class runs late and you need to close? Or an inspector comes? You can't have people getting sick or walk into a dirty, dusty studio. Then they add it to a review, now you're really screwed. Everything is about presentation and first impressions. Do you think I enjoy getting on a step ladder to dust the top of the bookshelves? I don't. But it has to be done."

"Greg wouldn't need a stepping stool. Just get him to do it." Calvin turned his head to side and eyed her with a hand on his hip. She crossed her arms. "I don't remember asking for the inspirational brother today."

"Welp you got him and the supplies he bought you to keep here. After this, you're on your own." He turned back towards the door and turned around. "Also, don't ask mom to pay for a company to clean, she already paid the studio rent for a year. She is retired now."

Casey rolled her eyes harder. He was right. "Yea yea, okay. Thanks Calvin for the cleaning stuff."

He smiled. "You're welcome! We, especially Gemini, are looking forward to the launch date. Have you settled on one yet? She wants to sign up for the first class. Do you have a website?"

Casey shook her head. "Yo! One step at a time. The poles literally got here like, yesterday. I can't decide on anything right now. I don't even know how to decorate this place. I need alcohol so the poles don't rust." She slammed her head in her hand. "I can't do this shit. This was a horrible idea." Her eyes started to well up again. "How am I going to run this place and do school at the same time? I should've never told mom about this idea. I don't think I even want to go to school. I'm just fucking bored. Who wants to sit in a classroom? Am I even bored or dissatisfied with my life? Omg I really ruined that girls hands and got fired from that salon."

He sighed. "Fuck I remember that. Didn't she get like second degree burns?"

"Every time I've tried to do *anything* on my own, I fuck it up." She quivered her lip.

Calvin walked back across the room with a compassionate look on his face. "Fine, I'll help. Just please don't cry okay?"

Casey sniffled and weakly smiled. "Thank you big brother, I won't forget your support."

"Just put some gloves on okay? Mom spoiled you rotten. I know your still scared of messing up your *delicate* hands."

She grabbed some gloves. "Yes, your fiancé already told me too. And yes I want soft hands, that's why I do a hand mask every now and then." They laughed together.

They did a deep clean of the space. While Calvin focused on the bathroom, Casey wiped down the poles and cleaned the glass mirror and windows. She made a mental note to create a checklist of what needed to be completed on the closing shift and in bi weekly deep cleans.

"I need to go by the store, do you need anything?" Calvin asked.

"Yea some curtains. I'll still pay for lunch and have it delivered here. Are wings cool?"

"Yes! Get me uh honey lemon pepper. I should be treated for the work I have endured for the 'princess Grant'." She threw a dirty paper towel at him as he ran out.

Calvin returned with a front door mat, curtain rod and blackout curtains. The food came a few minutes after. They ate their food as she caught him up on the run in with Denver.

"So you met him at the retreat in Colorado. That was a minute ago."

"It was. But we remembered each other. Whole time, I thought he was a white man, but he's mixed. I should've known since I know what he's swinging," She winked and he gagged. They finished eating and threw their trash away outside. She walked in again, checked behind the door and the bathroom. "All clear."

I need a security system she reminded herself.

After she pulled in the curtains and locked the door. She pulled on it and made sure it stayed locked. Hanging out with Calvin was fun. She couldn't help but to annoy him. She decided to call her mom and see if she was busy. Mama answered on the first ring. "My sweet Casey how is my darling?"

"Hey Mama how are you?"

"I'm good I'm just about to take a nap."

"Oh okay. Welllll I just wanted to give you a little entrepreneurial update. Calvin came over to help me clean the studio. It's really coming together! I'm even going to make a cleaning checklist and all that. Calvin bought some curtains too."

"Look at my little girl stretching out on her own. I'm so proud of you already. You're going to be successful not matter what."

Casey smiled to herself as she walked to her car and unlocked it, then set in the driver's seat. "Thanks Mama."

CHAPTER 7

CUE THE FAMILY FEUD MUSIC. "Goooood afternoon Helping Human Helpers! Are you ready for a game of feud! I'm your host Brain. Welcome to your Southern Sumitt! Today we have the Texas Finance Executives versus the Mississippi HR Executive Team!"

Yes he was an entertainer and comedian. Brian traveled to different corporate conferences, restaurants and bars to give a 'clean' fun show or raunchy, with approval. He had a contract with Helping Human Helpers, the biggest HR company in the country, as an employee engagement consultant. Or in regular terms, help people have fun with their co-workers during the workday by being funny and charming. The perfect cross between leading team-building exercises and people actually enjoying it.

A different department was in charge of building the agenda, arranging seats and picking the company approved games. Denver just came in with his microphone, smile and ball of energy. Sometimes it was trivia or Family Feud. In his heart, he wanted to be a stand up comedian, but hadn't tried a true stand up routine. He had mastered the craft of making people smile by being silly. A game is a game and they are meant to be fun. He approached each contestant with swagger and a smile.

In the end, it's a win win.

Not all of his work was done with HHH, though. As a freelancer he was also able to own all of his work and material. Atlanta would be the perfect place to set roots since it was conference central and HHH headquarters.

All he had to do was keep this sensual online persona, Country Cheeks, hidden. There weren't any extreme videos of him sucking three dicks at the same time, but there are definite videos with him only wearing chaps or satisfying himself in his favorite cowboy hat.

Then Casey crossed his mind. How would she even feel if he told her? He missed how Denver rolled out off her tongue. When he was around her, he forgot his own name, since she still called him the nickname she came up with at the retreat, in Denver of course.

When he was finished with the day, smiling, show boating and shaking hands, he was headed to his hotel room when an attendee approached him in front of the elevator. He had on a dark red polo with black dress slacks with light blonde hair.

"Hey man! Great game! That was the most fun I've had at one of these things. They're usually more stuffy. WOMP WOMP, metrics! WOMP WOMP spend less money!"

"Your welcome man, gotta smile through it." Denver said staring at the button, hoping that was the end of the conversation.

"You know what? I feel like I've seen you somewhere. Do you do commercials? Movies?" Denver's eyes grew wide as he frantically pressed the button faster. The only work he's done in front of the camera involved his ass being out while doing chores around the house.

"No I can't say that I have."

The man rubbed his chin. Ding. The elevator finally came and they stepped in. They selected their floors and rose up.

"I know! I follow you, You're Country Cheeks! I've been following you for a while man. You cleaned your kitchen in nothing but boots and straw hat! You have the best angles, too. I dreamed about you man."

The stranger began to size him up and it made Denver *extremely* uncomfortable.

"Are you open to more fun? Can I hire you for the night?" The man licked his thin pink lips.

Denver coughed as the door opened on his floor, "I'm sorry but I'm straight. Not the in denial kind of way, but I'm only sexually attracted to women. But, uh, thanks for watching." He quickly stepped out and high stepped to his room, slowly looking back to make sure he wasn't being followed. He understood being recognized in public. Denver forgot that most of his 100,000 subscribers were in the Atlanta area.

Even though he said women, he was really only attracted to Casey. Her intoxicating fragrance was a mix of cinnamon and peppermint; her long wavy hair, her determination to fulfill her dreams no matter the obstacles and just... her.

Even when they met at the retreat, she had a certain 'I don't give a fuck' glow. He loved it and his goal was to make a plan and ride with it. But Casey was determined to grow and better herself and her business. He couldn't wait to sign up for classes when he could. Even though he couldn't always fly to Atlanta on a whim, he was constantly learning about her and never wanted to stop. He missed her and needed to see her.

Immediately he took out his phone and texted Casey to see if she was available that night for a date. She thankfully said yes as long as it was a 'friendly' date. He started arranging his outfit, ironing his pants, unable to control his giddiness of seeing the woman he cared for in a matter of hours.

He had the perfect plan.

Even if it didn't sweep her off her feet, he wanted her to do something with her.

CASEY HOPPED out the shower and started getting dressed, taking the rods out of her hair. It had been 4 days since she'd seen or heard from Denver and she honestly missed him. *I'm not blowing up his phone though.* When he randomly asked her out on a bookstore date she actually felt excited about seeing him again. *Disgusting, he's so obsessed with me and I love and hate it.* She decided a matching periwinkle tennis skirt long sleeve set with all white low top Nikes was the perfect outfit.

When she arrived at the bookstore, it sat on a busy street, cars, shops, people eating at tables on the sidewalk. The familiar metropolitan city buzz of Midtown Atlanta that warmed her heart. Denver jogged to her. But he didn't lose his breath until he eyed her body.

"My my," he whispered in a drawl licking his bottom lip.

"Eyes up here, country boy."

He had on a forest green sweater with dark blue jeans. The sweater really exposed his firm muscular shoulders that made her feel safe, warm and fuzzy. She hoped this night led to her laying in his arms.

"Well this country boy is sorry for his behavior on Sunday. I didn't mean to leave that quick, I was just surprised. Work got busier than usual and I meant to text you. I'll support you in any and everything, as a good friend of course." He said with a wink.

She met his eyes, "Mm that's fine. I accept your apology." She finally took in what he was wearing, and those jeans that showed off his butt perfectly. Oh how her hands were gonna be all over that ass tonight.

"Eyes up here Georgia peach," he said leading her to the storefront. As he opened the door for her, he quickly kissed her cheek. "Oops sorry," he said sarcastically.

Casey blushed, actually blushed in public. She couldn't hide the smirk that grew on her face as they walked into the store.

"Hey! Welcome to Virginia Highlands, any book in particular your looking for?"

The woman had a nice smile, but Casey was awestruck as she scanned the walls, taking in the view of the two level bookstore. The staircase was right in the center, going straight down with more bookshelves. To the left, were vinyl's and a sitting area. "Wow it's bigger in here than I thought." She whispered.

The top level was filled with people silently walking and scanning the displays. The floor creaking under each step. She was in love. "I'm looking for the smuttiest, nastiest book you have."

The young woman chuckled as Denver tried to hide his laugh with a cough. "This is our romance section here. I'd recommend these two books. But if you like fantasy, try this one."

Casey hummed to herself. "Thank you!"

As Casey was picking up books and reading the summaries, Denver placed his hand on her hip. "I'm going to check out downstairs."

She nodded and he gave her a quick kiss on the cheek. Even though she knew he wasn't standing next her, watching her, anymore. She missed him. She missed his warmth, the way his eyes smoldered when they connect with hers. The random cheek kiss! Now a bookstore splurge? He's purposely trying to check her boxes.

And he was.

She noticed a children book on the main display, a black ballerina. She had afro puffs and a wand in her hand with a smile on her chocolate face. She was even wearing a tutu with tights that matched *her* skin tone. Casey stared at the book for awhile. A strange emotion stirred in her chest. Nostalgia? Hope? Grateful for change? She slowly walked towards the picture book and picked it up. The pages were drawn beautifully. "You are coming home with me." She said to herself.

THEY MADE it back to her condo an hour or so later since they were starting to close and Denver was carrying two totes of books.

"Are you cool with me fixing something for dinner?"

Casey kicked her shoes off and grabbed her bag. "Of course you can! I will be heads down in this book."

He chuckled. "Go ahead baby."

She effortlessly lifted on her toes and did a pirouette into a grand leap as she grabbed her book and blanket then stretched on the couch. When the blanket was to her chest she glanced at Denver, his head down into a bowl. Focused.

"What are you making?" She asked opening the bright covered book.

"Something you will love," he said with a smile.

She was already in the third chapter when Denver placed a bowl of steaming hot spicy Cajun chicken and shrimp pasta in front of her. "For the lady," he said in a British accent.

"Thank you," she replied in her regular voice putting the bookmark back in her book. She moaned when she took the first bite. It wasn't too spicy, but just enough to coat her tongue.

This was the kind of dish that made a woman say yes to a cooking man.

"Do you like it?"

"This is so delicious. I love it. It has just enough kick but I'm not sticking my head under the sink faucet." They laughed as Denver sat at her feet with his bowl.

"I need to have you cook more often. You haven't failed in the kitchen yet."

He chuckled, "I don't fail at much. Just some things."

"What's that?" Casey asked wiping her mouth.

"Winning over your heart for good."

She chuckled. When they finished eating, Casey offered to wash the dishes. Denver refused and told her to keep reading. He connected his phone to the Bluetooth speaker and began playing music.

He joined her on the couch with his book in hand, brushing his finger tips on her thighs. "*Love Jones*" by Leon Thomas filled the air.

"If you keep touching me like that, I'm going to get even hornier than this book is making me."

"Open your legs then."

Casey looked up from her book. "Huh?"

"Keep reading that scene in that smutty book of yours and open your legs. I can help." He flashed his 'Can't say no' grin. She couldn't say no if she tried. He always looked good, but even better between her thighs. When his teeth bit down on his bottom lip, her spine warmed. She pulled down her skirt, followed shortly after her smoke grey lace thong.

"You look so sexy baby."

He scooted down the couch and kissed her inner thigh as she shuddered, whispering the words of the book to herself to stay focused. He lightly kissed the way to her glistening center. Her knees shook when his tongue flattened against her core, curling and twisting. When he started stroking her with it she groaned, tightening as she slowly rode his tongue. Denver groaned his satisfaction as she began to bounce.

The male character was now fisting his fiancés hair as he growled in her ear from behind, giving her everything he had in strokes.

When he began sucking her sweetness she squealed again. "Keep reading," he growled. She panted as she read of how pleased with how wet his lovers pussy was. Denver's tongue slipped all over her, her knees buckled against his head. Every time she tried to scoot away, he dove deeper.

Casey grabbed her bookmark and threw it in the book. "I can't, not when your licking me up like this. Shit."

She tossed the book on the side table and quickly brushed her nails through his hair, scratching his scalp. He moaned and latched onto her with his bottom lip right as she climaxed. With every orgasm, the nerve endings around her body intensified. The goosebumps on her fingertips were so alive it was like they were shooting out beams of light. She gripped the arm behind her and exhaled as he rose above her, licking his lips.

"Mm that's a dessert I'd choose over the main course any day."

He unbuckled his pants and threw them on the ground. Her bottom lip dropped when his dick bounced, pointing directly at her. "You want me to tear those walls apart?"

"Please," she groaned. He teased her with his head, drawing small circles. When she growled at him, he smoothly entered. Her nails settled on his lower back as he stroked, lifting her legs with each thrust. Once her toes were pointed to the ceiling, he started going even faster. He was amazed by how her breast shook with each thrust, the way her lip quivered.

Suddenly, she grabbed his shoulders and pulled him to the couch. He laughed as she stood up and positioned herself on top of him, a leg on each side. Just as she lowered herself, his hands squeezed her waist, his thumbs brushing up her hour glass. They groaned together as she rode him. Her hair brushed past her ass as Denver's hands massaged her breast slowly. The whimper that escaped her lips was a noise she had never made before. Then he grabbed her shoulders, to keep her close. He pumped into her as her body bounced in excitement. She was unable to contain the scream and her nails digging into his back.

She knew he loved that shit from his determined gaze. She was in a zone filled with bliss, euphoria. This was the connection she wanted. When he hit her spot she squirmed. He grabbed her chin to look at him. His hazel eyes digging deeper into her soul. He lightly kissed her pouted lips as his finger tips brushed her spine.

She rolled her hips faster as his hands covered hers, guiding his hands all over her body. Up her arms, down her chest, in her hair. She felt a growl grow from his chest as his hands squeezed her hips.

"Shit, oh shit," he whispered.

Casey bent down and kissed him as he finished. It wasn't until she looked up that she remembered they were on the couch. Well a flat surface, was a flat surface.

When Denver returned to her with the hot wet towel, she tried to not drip. She chuckled as he placed the towel gently between her legs and wiped away their juices.

"So I leave tomorrow morning to go back home. I wish I didn't have to, though. If I wasn't such as asshole, we would've had more time together."

She nodded, trying to not look disappointed. "It's okay. Your coming back for my birthday right?"

"Of course, I wouldn't miss it. Now that I know about it."

"Good," she lightly shoved his shoulder. "You won't ghost me now, right?"

He caught her hand and kissed her fingertips, "No ma'am. I couldn't and wouldn't."

The next morning, he texted her when he made it to the airport and boarded his flight. When the acceptance hit that he wasn't in town, she was melancholy. She should've reached out to him more, but she refused to chase him.

Her birthday was only a few days away and she would survive without his dick.

CHAPTER 8

CASEY ANSWERED Denver's FaceTime as she was pole conditioning, knees to chest while being three feet in the air, which was not an easy feat. She reapplied the liquid chalk on her hands and hopped back on, counting out loud. She was feeling the burn everywhere but kept pushing through the counts. She could feel the tightness from her core all the way to her lower back.

"You've got great control Case, I know your core is something serious." She chuckled as she hopped down and rubbed her stomach and back with a grimace.

"Ugh!" she said with a sigh, laying on the ground in front of the camera, rolling over to be eye to eye. They started texting more the day after he left. Most days it was a good morning text and check in, then they Facetimed every few days. Each time, Casey was looking more forward to hearing from him.

"So what are you working on?" He asked, sitting on his couch working on his laptop.

"There's this move I've been trying to get down. I'd basically be doing a spin, then flip in the air, and catch myself with my knees. Then I slide down into a split."

His eyes widened, "That sounds dangerous."

She brew out air, "That's cause it is! I've already face planted on this mat twice. So I'm working on my core to build up my strength some more. What have you been up to?"

"Well right now I'm researching. I have a *Bridgerton* Trivia night. I was invited to host. If they like me, they may give me a contract for a couple weeks which would be consistent money. So I'm looking for fun facts and creating some jokes to stand out."

"So being funny, is basically your job."

"And entertaining. I do smaller gigs on the side to help keep money in the door. But I make enough to keep flying out to see you." Casey turned away from the camera to smile, she didn't want him to know she was smitten. "Why do you like pole fitness? I don't think I've ever asked you."

She took a deep breath and turned to look at her ceiling. "It makes me feel like I'm flying. It's a beautiful form of art that actually takes practice to master. I grew up taking dance classes so I'm used to dancing for long hours or auditioning with 100 other girls in the room. But maybe two, would look like me. Pole fitness helped me bring dancing back to my heart. My degree is in dance, and it just mixes well with it. It's also sexy and fun rather than being yelled at in French."

"Well, I'm happy you get to do what you love. I think the studio is going to be great for you. I know it'll be a success." He smiled so hard that his eyes crinkled. He looked like he meant what he said.

Casey's mind wandered to the overwhelming tasks that still needed to be done for her business. So she weakly said, "Yea."

CASEY WOKE up to her phone ringing. She answered sleepily, "Mornin' Mom."

"Good morning, sweetheart!" Her mom said excitedly on the other line. Then she started singing Stevie Wonder's version of Happy Birthday as she sleepily danced along, rubbing her eyes as her mom extended the 'aaayyy' on the last note.

"Thank you Mama."

"You're welcome. My gift should arrive shortly. I hope you like it! Sorry I can't make it to your party tonight."

"Mom it's fine. This isn't a party where you really want your mom there."

Mama chuckled, "I guess so. But either way enjoy your day. You have grown so much whether you see it or not. I'm so proud of you."

"Thank you, you have a good day too."

As Casey was walking out of the bathroom, there was a knock at the door. She took the day off, in her mind it's illegal to work on your birthday, but she was sure Coraline was going to leave emails for her to read that had nothing to do with her.

Today was about self care and relaxation, no business. She already had an appointment at the spa getting a massage and her nails done, some shopping for her outfit tonight then a good nap before her party. She yawned her way to the door and looked through the peep hole, flowers?

When she opened the door, a large bouquet of roses greeted her. She smiled widely. After accepting them from the delivery guy, she closed the door and walked back to the kitchen. Were these from her mom? A secret admirer? She picked up the arrangement and carefully placed it on her counter. Then noticed the card.

Happy 26th Birthday!
You are special, loved and I hope you receive everything
you dream of this next year of your life.

See you tonight.

Your friend,

Denver (Brian)

SHE BLUSHED and lightly touched the roses. She was never good with keeping plants alive, but she knew she would take great care of these flowers. She tried to not think too much about the 'your friend' comment. Even though it was true. Denver was serious about not pushing too hard, but it was starting to annoy her. She didn't care that he wanted to claim her. She was only turning 26. She made it this far technically single and planned on going further.

What made the difference, would be if he was sending another 'friend' flowers. How could he have time to entertain another woman? *Men make time for the things they want and plan it out to a tee.*

She called him. "Good morning birthday girl!" He said excited. "Did you get the flowers?"

"Yes I did! I wanted to call and say thank you. They are cute as fuck." She took a sniff, they were indeed fresh and fragrant. She heard slams and grunts in the background. "Are you at the gym?"

He exhaled, "Yea I'm on the leg press right now. My plane doesn't leave for a couple hours so I wanted to get a workout in before I started working you out tonight."

She bit her lip. "Mmm I like the sound of that. Text me when you're boarding and when you land so I can pick you up. I hope you didn't make hotel arrangements."

"I did. But I can easily cancel. You're sure that you want to be around me all weekend?"

She gasped. "Of course I do! You need to be ready to be on-go all night, mister. I've got some ideas for you."

"Mmm, yes ma'am." He said in a country accent. They said their goodbyes and hung up the phone. Then she squealed. Actually squealed.

I need to get my day started and my shit together.

She got dressed, set her Uber and prepared to receive love and pampering all day. The 'Happy Birthday' messages already started to pour in on social media and texts from her family and friends.

CASEY SAT in front of her vanity in the bathroom. She was trying not too look at her phone every 5 minutes. Denver said he'd get an Uber instead of making her sit in traffic to the airport on her birthday. After she came back from the spa, she sat on the couch and watched a few episodes of *College Hill: Celebrity Edition* to kill some time. As much as she tried to fight it, she missed him and was excited to see him.

There was an urgent knock at the door. She ran on her toes to the door, looked in the peephole and swung it open. Denver stood there with a cheesy grin, his suitcase in one hand and one hand behind his back.

"There's my birthday girl!" He threw multi colored confetti around her as she laughed. Nobody has ever thrown confetti for her and she found it cute.

"Awwwwwwww and Hi! I was not expecting that." She laughed as she spun around in the sparkles.

He entered and placed his bag down. As soon as his hands were free, Casey jumped into his arms and he caught her, nuzzling his face in her neck as she squeezed his shoulders. "I missed you! The entrance was pretty spectacular."

"I missed you too, you look beautiful. You're welcome, I will sweep it up, too. I didn't mean to make a mess." With her arms rested around his neck, brushing her thumbs against his brown curls. Denver securely held her. They leaned in and kissed slowly, melting deeper and deeper in the kiss. She slipped her tongue in his mouth with a moan as she lightly touched his face. He slowly walked to the couch and sat down as she stayed on his lap, their lips never separating.

"I've missed your kisses so much." Casey said breathlessly in his ear.

"I missed kissing you too. I thought I couldn't breathe without your lips on mine."

His hands rubbed her back as he kissed her collar bone. It felt like his hands where in six different places at once and she loved it. Craved it. Needed it.

She moaned and breathed into his ear then asked, "Why did you sign those beautiful roses as a friend?"

His lips paused on her nape. "Do you want to be more baby? Are you ready for that commitment to me? You just have to tell me because you already have me wrapped around your finger." He kissed the gap between her breast, his nose soft against her skin. "I'm not rushing just asking." He kissed the bottom of her collar bone.

She sighed, running her nails on his scalp, lightly kissing his head. She wasn't ready. She didn't need to be locked down if she got the benefits already. Why be claimed by one person? "Can you give me a little more time?" She kissed his ear. "You've been so patient already, friend." She whispered.

He breathed in her skin, "I'll always be here."

She reached her hand toward his pants, scratched her nails against the seam. He growled. "You like that?" She asked breathy.

"It doesn't take much for you to undo me, Case. I'm yours."

She unbuttoned his pants and slowly brought the zipper down. He lifted his hips and pulled his pants and briefs down. She got off his lap and got on her knees. She licked her lips as she looked up at him, massaging his hard dick. A shudder went down his spine as he laid his head back. She smiled. She slowly licked his tip and lowered her mouth onto him.

"Fuck," he groaned. "You look so good sucking me baby damn."

She started going faster and faster and Denver's back arched. She placed his hand behind her neck which made him groan louder. He slowly fucked her face as she rubbed circles on his gap, her lips wrapped around him, her throat full of him. His legs started to spread and shake. "I'm about to -." She shoved him to back and pressed on the gap. He grunted and panted as the warmth went down. She finished with a loud slurp and pop.

She stood up and wiped her mouth, his head rested on the head of the couch. "Fuck. I wasn't expecting that."

"I know, but it's my birthday and I get to do whatever I want."

"Very true sweetheart. I'm going to hop in the shower and start getting ready for tonight. What time do we need to leave?"

Casey looked up at her clock. "At least an hour which should be plenty of time for me to put on makeup, decide what I'm wearing and roll a blunt."

After Denver came out of the shower, she was in the closet arranging outfits. "I can't decide on if I should wear a mini skirt. It's a lingerie party so I need to be sexy, but not too revealing. Everybody is not going to see my nipples for free, just a tease."

He wrapped a towel around his waist and walked into the closet, behind her. His body heat made goosebumps appear on her arms. "What do you want the outfit to say?" He asked.

She thought about it. "I want to break necks when I walk in. Everyone needs to drool when I walk by and compliment my titties."

She picked up the neon yellow halter top skin tight dress with the open back. "Try this with some stilettos."

She nodded her head. "I like that, I'm gonna try it on. But you can't peak." She smacked his butt and ushered him out of the closet, closing the door.

THE UBER BLACK stopped at the front door of, Green Envy Gentlemen's club, one of the best strip clubs in Atlanta. The line was wrapped around the building with beautiful people wearing skimpy lingerie to trench coats. It was known for having the sweetest Georgia Peaches, the best wings, and roof-twerking dancers. Thanks to the training program Casey implemented after accepting the role of Executive Trainer. She would host pole Zoom classes so performers can practice, get new move ideas across the country and not have to physically be at work.

The car door opened and Denver kissed her hand and exited. He wore a Fenty robe with matching black shorts. Casey had to squeeze her fists together from smacking his ass as they walked out. He looked fine as fuck. Security extended their hand in the SUV and helped her out of the car. The red carpet waiting for her. She waved to everyone in line as they screamed back various happy birthdays. She skated through security and waited at the club doors. The DJ turned down the music as Casey stood at the door, the red carpet out waiting for her. Then he yelled, "Grant Royalty in the house! It's sweet baby Princess Casey! Happy sexy 26th Birthday!" Then the speaker blasted, "*Sexyy Please*" by Sexyy Red.

She strutted down the carpet, performers and bottle girls lined on both sides. When she spotted her friend Sky, she stuck her tongue out and twerked while she smacked her ass. Casey slowly winded her hips and flipped her hair. The room erupted into cheers.

The lights were on her. She looked perfect. Her face was beat. She looked thick, delicious and chocolate like a KitKat in yellow wrapping. She slowly strutted all the way to her section, Gemini, Denver and Coraline waited for her. Denver stood up and extended his hand to her to help her up the stairs, admiration and lust showing in his eyes. She pursed her lips, then licked her top lip as she sat down.

He leaned into her ear, "Just wait till we get home. I'm tearing that off of you."

She lifted the corner of her lips, "Mmm are you sure?" She brushed her nails across his chin, playing with his chin. He looked at her lips and back in her eyes.

"I guess we'll see." She leaned and kissed him, in public. His eyes were in a daze and she smiled back.

"Uhh don't forget were here." Coraline said with a cough. Casey turned over her shoulder and smiled with a wink.

"How can I not be sexy on my 26th sis?"

Coraline shrugged and handed her a wrapped box. "Here's your gift, since I gave you a day off today." Coraline wore dark blue silk pajama pants set. Her hair gelled back into a ponytail.

Casey squealed as she tore the paper, then an orange box appears. Her jaw dropped. "Bitch is this what I think it is?!"

"Open it and see."

Casey opened a large orange box to a Hermes bag, a

Garden Party 49 Voyage bag. She had been eyeing this bag for awhile. "Oh this is sexy. I love it thank you, sis!" She got up and hugged her sister.

"Well now I feel like I should've given my gift first." Gemini said with a laugh. She pulled out a gift bag with wrapping paper. Casey opened it to a journal, gift card and a makeup bag."

"I still love these Gem." Casey got up and hugged her too. Gemini was wearing a lace bra with silk pajama shorts.

"Sorry Calvin couldn't make it. You know how he is,"

"Girl you don't have to apologize for him. I know Calvin hates the club."

After her gifts were taken to the back and locked away, some of the girls come back and brought drinks and started flirting with them. One in particular wouldn't leave Coraline's ear and started giving her a lap dance. With the way they smiled at each other, they either knew each other or were about to get more acquainted. It wasn't long before they left for the VIP room.

"Where is the best place for me to sit and not seem like a creep?" Gemini asked looking around the club.

Casey chuckled, "You can sit in front of the stage. They are here to be admired, just no touching unless they say it's okay. And you're a girl so they would probably be okay with it."

"Everyone is so beautiful, I want to faint. I think I see the seat I want."

"I'll come with." Gemini and Casey went down to sit in front of the main stage. It had three poles and three performers, two were spinning on the same pole. Gemini's jaw dropped as she placed dollar bills on the stage. Casey was throwing the money on the stage while praising them.

Gemini had one drink in her hand, and the other holding

her stack of ones. When someone dropped into a split then looked her in the eye with a sly smile. She sighed dreamily. "I think I fell in love again. Casey they are amazing! I could never be that balanced and look that sexy doing it."

Casey laughed. "Come to a couple of my classes when I open my studio and I'll teach you. But it definitely isn't easy. I'm personally not a fan of floor work, but it has a strong effect."

"I wouldn't even be able to walk in those shoes. Are those 8 inches?"

"Probably even more," Casey chuckled. "You can do anything with a little practice sis." She threw bills in the air, raining on the girls. "I'm going back to the section, want to come?"

Gemini nodded, but was locked eyes with performer who just unsnapped her top. Her breast bouncing from the release with gold pierced nipples. "Actually, just one more song. For her."

Casey strutted back to the section, when another drink appeared in her hand. She took a sip, smiled and raised her cup to the bar where the girls smiled and winked back.

Denver had his arm around Casey's shoulders as they sat in the section. A couple of girls approached him for dances but he turned every single one down. What was his type? They had chocolate, vanilla, caramel, tall, short, thick and fit. But he turned them all down. Casey was the one he wanted.

"Denver, it's my birthday. Why aren't you dancing with anyone?"

He looked surprised she asked. "Because I've got the best one under my arm and I don't want to be disrespectful."

Casey scoffed and waved a girl over. She was wearing a 2-piece emerald green thong and bikini top. "Sky!"

Sky turned her head and walked over. "Yes boss?"

"Don't call me that! My friend Denver here," Casey

brushed her hand on his chest, "Has been acting shy all night. Can you do me a favor and dance with him?"

Sky eyed Denver up and down and smiled. "Of course I can. Wanna watch?"

Casey took a sip of her drink. "You know I do."

Sky opened her hand. "Don't worry Mr. Denver, I won't bite." He looked at Casey and grabbed Sky's hand and stood up. Sky spun around and showed her body off to him. Her coffee skin glittered as she guided him to the nearby wall.

She swayed her hips side to side against him as he exhaled. "That's right just relax." Sky said seductively. She began to twerk and Denver couldn't help but to get hard. She moved her ass against him to the music, his shoulders slowly relaxing. "I didn't know you had rhythm Mr. Denver."

He did a half smile, "Thanks."

"And I feel that you enjoyed my dance too."

His face was dark red.

"Oh don't go back to being shy. If you need ANYTHING else, just call me over."

He gave her a $50 and she winked.

Denver went back to the section and poured another glass of champagne starting to sweat. "See that wasn't so bad!" Casey said teasingly. "It was actually kind of sexy." She kissed his lips twice. "You don't need my permission, were still technically single so enjoy tonight."

His eyes shattered but he was trying to hide it. Casey noticed and didn't apologize for the true comment.

Sky came into the section, "Hey boss! Are you going to give us a little birthday dance?"

Gemini's jaw dropped as she turned toward her, "Oh my god. You have to! Even just for one song, pleaseee."

Casey rolled her eyes, "Yall know I don't want to get all

sweaty and shit. I just got my nails done and I don't want chalk on them."

"I'll pay to get them fixed," Denver said in her ear, kissing her lobe. He's seen her practice, but never on the stage.

Sky pulled Casey out of her seat. "You don't have to do anything on the ceiling, just give us some cute spins."

Casey rolled her eyes and smiled, "I don't like bills being thrown at my pussy Sky. You know this, I'm there for the stage presence. The energy."

"Yes 'stage presence' and 'energy' you train us on how to do it. So you do it! It's your birthday go up there and have fun!"

Gemini and Sky pleaded to Casey while Denver's looked intrigued with raised eyebrows.

"Fine, but I'm not doing it in this."

Sky held her hand and pulled her through the **Staff Only** doors. "You know we have two outfits in the back with some space to stretch."

Casey went to the back dressing room and changed into a hot pink thong 2 piece. She borrowed a pair of heels and socks, not wanting to scuff her good shoes.

While stretching into a split, she thought about Denver. Was he okay? After she made the comment about being single, he had a look in his eye. She ignored it but saw the hurt. She looked at herself in the mirror. Her breasts were perfect and perky, her hair fell to her waist with fresh curls.

She texted Sky and said she was ready and the song to send to the DJ. She was behind the stage, waiting. She took a deep breath as she practiced her twerk doing more stretches. Then she heard the DJ, "Welcome to the stage, the birthday girl and Grant princess herself, Casey!"

She quickly applied the grip assistance on her hands and slowly strutted out to the beat of the music, letting it fill her. *"Blue Flame Ballet"* by Big Krit vibrated throughout the club.

The stage was filled with dark pink and midnight blue lights. She approached the middle pole, leaning against it, teasing the crowd with a slow grind of her hips. *I'm that bitch and I look fine as shit.* Then she grabbed the pole from behind and spun with her ankles crossed in front of her. When she let one hand go and did a flare kick, then spun a few times. She then made it look like she was walking in mid air. She made eye contact with Denver and he stared back at her in awe. Perfect. She brought her leg back in, hooked her knee and hung upside down with a sultry smile. She climbed with her knees towards the top of the 15 foot pole. The anticipation of the crowd was building.

When the beat picked back up, she went into an aerial deadlift. Her feet next to her head while she was upside down, holding on her hip. Smoke erupted from the back of the stage as she smiled to herself. *Hell yea.*

"The princess is dominating tonight yall! Throw them dollas in the air not on the stage!" Bills then flew in the air. She brought her legs back down with a slow spin, then dropped and caught herself 2 inches from the ground, the crowd gasped. She popped her head up, did a squat and sexily eyed the crowd, searching for Denver again. He moved closer to the stage, but kept his distance.

Casey body rolled all the way to the ground and got on her knees, swinging her hair behind her and her hands slowly caressing her breast. The crowd cheering again. She stood up and did a turn into a leap as she grabbed the next pole with a perfectly timed hair flip with the music. She loved incorporating her two styles with professional and sexy. After she freestyled more spins, she landed into a split and twerked as more money filled the air. As the song got towards the end, she got back on the pole and ended in another flare kick into a spin with arm up.

The DJ spoke in the mic again, "The teacher, the trainer,

the empire baby, give it up again for Casey! We love you and happy birthday girl!"

She blew a kiss to the DJ and the crowd, then gracefully walked backstage. Sky was there waiting, jumping up and down. "Bitch you fucking killed it! Had me feeling all horny and impressed. I know you be fucking the shit out of white boy."

Casey rolled her eyes as she wiped off her sweat and washed her hands. "Mmm hm but we don't go together. He also isn't white, well fully."

Sky made a face at her. "Oh okay get me together about your 'friend'."

"He's mixed." Casey said shaking her head. "And don't make that face."

"Me? What face?" Casey gave her a deadpan stare and they laughed together.

"Alright I'll let you change and get back out there. You did great boss." Sky winked at her and left the room.

Casey returned to her section to an applause and awe. "Ahh! I was so scared when you did that drop. I thought your neck was gonna break," Gemini said.

"I've been practicing that trick, I still feel it." Casey said with a chuckle. "Have you seen Denver?"

Gemini shook her head, "No I lost him when you went on stage."

Coraline reappeared with Angel, hand in hand. She had a look on her face like she was in love. *This was the last place to have that look.* Casey tapped Gemini on her shoulder, "You see how sprung my sister looks right now?"

Gemini slowly turned to look at her and the woman she was speaking too. Their heads were so close together that it looked like they were kissing. "She does look sprung. That's how I've felt every 5 minutes since we've been here."

"She's talking to Angel. It's nothing new, but they always leave it here, to my knowledge. Angel is her favorite girl, probably only. She literally comes here twice a week when she's working just to spend time with her. Angel is also on the payroll so nothing like special treatment from the CEO."

"Ooo okay. It's giving favoritism." Gemini said sipping her drink. "I hope she keeps her eyes open, you never know. But if she likes her, why don't they just date?"

"Angel is married, Coraline is a workaholic. It's complicated."

Gemini nodded. "Seems like a few things are complicated tonight." Casey clinked her glass with Gemini's and took a sip.

From across the room, Casey noticed Greg at the crowded bar, whispering to the man next to him. She knew that beard and belly anywhere. They made eye contact and he raised his glass towards her. The man next to him turned his head to here and smiled. Oh he's *fiooe*. He's Damson Idris fine. *I need to get my ass over there.* "I'm gonna be right back," she said in Gemini's ear.

"Bet," Gemini looked towards the bar too. "Ahh look at Greg with his thick ass. I didn't know he was going to be out tonight."

"Nah I'm headed to the nigga next to him." She said standing adjusting her dress.

"Hell yea," with a high five.

Casey flipped her hair and reapplied her lip gloss. She did a room scan for Denver and he was getting a lap dance. *Perfect he's occupied.*

She made it to the bar, looking as delicious as she could. "Happy birthday jit!" Greg shouted.

She rolled her eyes, "Wow I've been grown but thanks."

"I'm just messin' with you damn. Great performance too, you busy later?" He asked brushing his hand against hers.

"I am busy for you, but not him." She licked her top lip while looking at him, "Who's your friend here?"

"You don't recognize me Casey Cake?" The man said in a deep baritone voice. She could hear his voice over the music or anything happening behind her. "It's Ayden Jones."

Her brain did a reset.

Ayden Jones.

Her first boyfriend, first kiss Ayden Jones. What was he doing back? "Wow. Um. I didn't know you were back in town." She started rubbing her elbow. No wonder why he didn't look familiar, she hadn't seen him in 8 years.

"Yea I just finished school and shit."

School?

"Oh that's what your calling jail? School?"

The last Casey heard, Ayden was in Fulton County jail for drug possession with intent to sell and looking at possibly 5 years. She was heartbroken when he got locked up. His court date was during her high school graduation, what could've been their high school graduation.

They were in the same grade and Ayden really was smart, but too smart for his own good. His strongest class was chemistry. Casey never liked or understood the periodic table, but Ayden had it memorized at 15. On the outside, he appeared as tough as possible, but she knew what was under his armor. A smart black man that made a few wrong choices. She begged him to stop dealing back then. Him and Greg started working together when they were 16. Once they found a plug that would sell to them. But Greg only wanted to sell weed, Ayden wanted something heavier. Stronger. That was what got him in trouble.

He chuckled. "I was only in jail for 18 months gah damn. It aint that serious. I got out early on good behavior though. Anyways I deal with it legally now."

Her face twisted. "How do you deal drugs legally A?"

He smiled the pearly smile again. Now she saw him, really saw him. The man she loved, or used to love. They never did go all the way. Back then, Casey was scared of anything more than a kiss or titty grab. Teenage pregnancy was too real and she never wanted kids. You can't always book auditions if you're pregnant. At least, that was where her head was back then.

He continued talking, "I'm a pharmacist. I just finished medical school and came back home to celebrate with my folks. Greg and I came out to celebrate. I was not expecting to see yo fine ass though." He eyed her up and down as he drank her in. "You still fuckin wit a nigga?"

Casey pressed her lips together to hide her blush. She knew she was fine, she's always been fine. But hearing it from his lips woke up her spirit. "Thank you. And yea I still fuck with you. Did you see my performance?"

His eyes danced over her body again, "I did. My favorite move was when you hooked your leg around the pole and hung upside down. I was like gah damn. You look good as hell though. I'm glad you doin good." He opened his arms for a hug and a cheesy grin grew on her face as she walked up to him and wrapped her arms into his, his back right under her finger tips. She couldn't stop herself from slowly brushing her hands down his back.

Ayden hummed in her ear, then kissed it. "I missed you."

"I missed you too. I'm glad to know your okay after all this time." As they started to separate, she was already missing how his body felt wrapped under her. *Oh that's what I need tonight.* "Do you want to look for a table and sit down?"

"I'd love the pleasure." Ayden said with the most charming smile.

A table wasn't far, he pulled her seat and she sat down. He

quickly took the seat across from hers. He opened his hand for hers and she took it without a second thought.

Then a familiar body started to appear closer and closer in her vision. Denver. *Oh yea opps.*

"Hey Casey," Denver said walking up to their table. He gave Ayden a questioned look but looked back at her. "Are you ready to head out?"

Ayden stood up from the table and extended his hand, "Wassup I'm Ayden. Casey and I go way back."

Denver shook his hand with an arched eyebrow. "Hey man. Casey, are you ready to go?"

She looked in between both. Denver was staring at her with his hands in his pockets, Ayden gave her a waiting glance. Who was she going to go home with?

"I'm going to hang out for a little while, Denver."

He nodded with a frown, not surprised. "Well my stuff is at your place, can I get your key?" Casey dug in her purse and handed them to him. "Happy birthday again," he said solemnly. Then Denver turned on his heels and walked away.

"What was that about?" Ayden asked.

Casey pressed her lips together, "Oh were just friends. He flew in for my birthday and is staying at my place."

Ayden's eyebrow arched, "He ain't your man?"

"Nah I'm single," she brushed her index finger against his ear. "What are you doing tonight though?"

"Nothin' is on my calendar. What's good?"

"Let's get outta here," she said with a wide smile.

She went back to her section and told Gemini and Coraline bye. "Where's Denver?" Gemini asked.

"He left already."

Gemini gave her a confused look, but didn't ask anymore questions. "Okay be safe. Text me when you get home."

Casey nodded and stuck her tongue out, Ayden came

behind her and placed a hand on the curve of her back. "You ready?" He asked.

She smiled, "Hell yea."

Gemini took a sip of her drink while she gave Coraline a look. Coraline looked at her unbothered.

"They all start to look the same." Coraline said with a shrug.

CHAPTER 9

AYDEN OPENED the door to his hotel room, and held it for Casey. She slowly strutted in the suite. The room was the size of a studio apartment. As she looked out of the window, he stood behind her, resting his hands on her waist. She slowly rocked her hips against his hardness. He hummed in her ear and squeezed her waist. "Whatchu want?"

She looked up at him, through her thick lashes. She lifted her head and kissed his lips. It was slow at first, but when he grabbed the back of her neck and drew small circles with his tongue, she melted, pulling herself impossibly closer to him, their tongues dancing on each other. She fisted his shirt and moaned, his hands now squeezing her ass. They rocked side to side as they swept each other up in the kiss.

She thought about the first time they kissed in the high school hallway. They always used the bathroom during 6th period and met in the stairwell around the corner from the computer lab. The foot traffic wasn't high and the classroom was empty. Ayden always kissed her like it was the last.

She loved it.

Tasting the desperation. It was the rush she always loved. Then she came back to the present when he gently kissed her color bone. She moaned as she put her head back, *perfect.* She eyed the large bed, slowly walking backwards towards it.

When the back of her legs hit it, Ayden chuckled. She sat on the bed looking up at him and he leaned into her. Her lips crashed onto his, forcing his mouth open with her tongue. As they kissed, she could not stay still. Her hands squeezed his arms and traveled down his back. He started to grind against her. She groaned as their nipples brushed each others charged skin.

"Please tell me you have condoms," she breathed.

He opened the nightstand drawer and grabbed one. He waved the condom between his fingers before he tore off the wrapper and sheathed himself. He bent down kissing her stomach, then her sweet lips. Her thighs began to shake as his tongue danced and twirled on her. Her hand rested on top on his head, her fingers digging in to his fro. As he slurped her, she began grinding on his face as he tongue plunged inside of her. "Put it in, fuck."

"Oh I'm taking too long baby?" Ayden asked between her legs.

"Yes," she breathed. He circled her clit with his nose then rose. His hands rested next to her head and eased inside of her.

She hooked her arms under his as he stroked her. "Fuck please don't stop."

"I won't."

Then he dug deeper with his hips, his hand fisting her hair as he moaned in her ear. She lifted her head and kissed him, hungrily; like his lips would save her from anything, everything.

There was history on his lips, time on his tongue.

His hand cradled her head, she squealed as he started pounding her. She whimpered on his lips as her nails pressed into his back. He kissed her begging lips, "You gonna keep takin all of me? Your pussy is drenched."

He pounded into her so fast she couldn't think. Then he lifted her legs up, her knees almost to her ears.

"I couldn't hear you. Can you take all of me? You're not quittin on me are you?" He smiled a devilish grin above her.

"Yes yes I can take it. Fuck your so deep."

He bent down and kissed her cheek, still holding her legs up. "I know, I'm bout to rearrange your shit." She locked eyes with him, seeing all the love she had hidden in herself finally release. The first man to break her heart was now taking her over the edge. She kissed his neck then bit him. The best representation of their relationship.

Lust and pain.

"Put that ass back in the air for me. Leme see that pussy."

Casey rolled on her stomach and twerked as he lifted her ass. He dove in, licking her lips as his thumb stroked her. Her hips buckled. He did one last suck and sat up. He stroked her from the side as he held open her cheeks.

"Denver," she whispered into the cover.

Ayden froze behind her. "Huh?" He smacked her ass. "Did you just say that niggas name? Oh hell nah."

Casey stumbled over her words. "N- no."

"Yes you did. But I'm about to remind you. Stand up." She slowly got off the bed and stood up. He walked up to her, gently holding her jaw. He traced her cheekbone to her ear, then turned her against the wall. "Put your hands on the wall." She obeyed. "You want to keep saying your other niggas name? Ight. I'm bout to fuck the shit out of you while you do."

Casey whimpered as Ayden spread her open again. He spit

on his dick and entered her again and again. Her nails scratching the wall, trying to support her from the power pushing behind her. Then a scream escaped from her throat as her body filled with heat and pressure.

Pure ecstasy.

CHAPTER 10

CASEY KNOCKED on her own front door. After a few minutes, Denver opened the door in a grey t shirt and his boxer briefs. His face looked flushed as they made eye contact.

She knew it was eight in the morning, the day after her birthday. Frankly, she didn't care how he felt right now. It was her life. She walked past him into her condo, the tension in the room thick. "How was your night?" He asked crossing his arms.

"It was great. What about yours?" The memory of Ayden grabbing her neck from the back, pounding her until her nails scratched the walls came in her mind.

He sat on the couch, "I didn't plan on getting embarrassed, but it was fine."

"How did I embarrass you? We are not a couple, Denver."

He stood back up, "Call me Brain. No more nicknames."

She furrowed her eyebrows. "Oh wow it's like that. I'm sorry I'm not ready for an exclusive relationship right now *Brian*. But I said we were single. Did you see me trippin seeing you dance and get lap dances? No. I was encouraging you to go out there. So no. You don't get to judge me for acting single."

"But we came together Case. I'm whole staying at your place. You dismissed me at the table in front of whoever that was."

She twisted her lips, "We arrived in the same vehicle yes. But it wasn't anything beyond that."

He walked to the window, his arms still crossed but the tension in his face started to loosen. "So everything about us tearing into each other last night was a lie. You made it seem like I was the only guy you wanted to be with."

Casey leaned on her counter, "I'm sorry I don't have a name for it. But I enjoy multiple relationships, okay? I don't see myself being tied to one person. Ever. Especially right now. I hadn't seen Ayden in years and I missed him. I didn't mean to ditch you, it just happened."

His shoulders rose and fell, "I get it." He headed to the bedroom, disappeared for a few moments and came back with joggers and a long sleeve on. "I'm going to take a walk and get some breakfast. Do you want anything?"

"Yea a cinnamon raisin bagel and hard boiled eggs." He put his wallet in his pocket. He walked past her, paused and then turned around. Her heart jumped because she wasn't sure how he still felt. Then he slowly bent down and kissed her cheek. "You don't want to kiss my lips anymore?"

A cold stare crossed over his eyes, "You haven't brushed your teeth yet." Then he closed the door.

So touchy. She pulled out her phone and saw Gemini texted her.

Gemini: I wasn't going to say anything at first, but I need the fucking tea

Casey: LMAO! Wyd on Sunday?

Gemini: I got tickets to this paint and sip
brunch. Want to come?

Casey: Of course!

Gemini: Bet I'll send you the details. See you
then sis!

CASEY LOVED HER MESSAGE

SHE TOOK a long and needed shower, brushed her teeth and combed through her hair. Ayden almost made her sweat out her body wave bundles. Maybe she could talk Calvin into washing and reinstall her sew in again. The waves weren't as defined right now so she moisturized and braided her hair into two braids.

When Denver came back, he had a large brown bag and a cup holder with coffee cups. "You didn't say what you wanted to drink, so I brought a raspberry tea."

Casey looked up at him from the couch from her book. She decided to put on her matching burgundy pajama short set since she wasn't planning to leave anytime soon.

He handed her the cup of tea and the bagel. "I want to apologize about how I acted. I know were aren't together and I can't claim you. I just... care about you a lot and I felt some type of way last night. I'm already here on limited time, but I get that I can't just spend it with you. Are you okay with me eating my breakfast here? I can change my flight to leave today instead of tomorrow."

Casey stood up and grabbed his hand. "Look, you don't have to leave. I was looking for you when I came back to the section. I saw you having a good time, so I wanted some too. Sorry that it made you feel some kind of way."

Denver nodded. They ate together and watched a reality show. When they finished, he started rolling two blunts.

"Why are you rolling two? I have cuties now? You don't want our lips on the same one?"

He chuckled, "No I wasn't going to light this one until later. That's if you still wanted to spend the rest of today with me."

"Yea I do, since you were a good boy and apologized."

"I'll always *try* to be a good boy. I just don't like when you catch someone elses eye."

She sighed, "I've literally known Ayden forever. We went to high school together and he was my long time crush. He was locked up for a minute and we fell out. It was a fucked up situation and all my dad's fault. Anyways," she said with a shrug. "I hung out with him and yea we fucked." She shrugged again.

"I get it," he mumbled. "Were single."

She stood up and opened the door to the porch and Denver followed.

He lit the joint just as Casey asked, "To change the subject, who is on your Mount Rushmore of music?"

He blew out the smoke. "Prince, Michael Jackson, Kendrick and Shaboozy."

Casey thought, "You know that's not too bad."

"Who is on yours?"

"Oh that's easy. Beyonce, Outkast, Usher, Ciara and honorable mention to Megan Thee Stallion."

Denver nodded in agreement. "That's literally 6 people but also great picks. What's your favorite Outcast album? ATLiens?"

"No but it's in my top 3. It's actually Aquemini. It's smooth and showed how well they balance each other out, sound wise and lyric wise." She pulled and blew the smoke out a few times then passed it to Denver. "Since we went to the bookstore, what kind of books did you like to read when you were younger?"

He thought about it while admiring the cars driving below them. "I didn't really read much as a kid. I just remember going to school and coming home to the ranch and taking care of the horses. I loved it no doubt. I just didn't get into reading until after college. I started getting into historical fictions and haven't let go since. I have a book on my nightstand that I pick up every now and then. But I wouldn't call myself an avid reader. But I can tell how much books mean to you, even though you don't say it."

He handed her the joint as she looked away. "Are you going to be able to keep your feelings out of this? I'm fine with dates but I don't want another situation like this morning."

Denver nodded, "I understand and I apologize again for overstepping your boundaries. My flight leaves early tomorrow so I'll be out of your hair soon. I just wanted us to hang out outside of your condo, that's all."

"Come on we can do something tonight. My mind is just drawing a blank."

"Well since were in Atlanta, what was one of the fun things you would do growing up?"

She looked outside of the window and giggled.

"You were egging houses weren't you?" he asked.

She laughed louder and he asked again. "So it's worse? You were recording dance videos on your school hallway?"

She stopped laughing and gave him a deadpan stare. "Don't judge me okay? How else would I post choreography on YouTube?"

Denver roared in laughter, with his hand on his belly. Then stepped to her. His smile. His cute smile, white teeth with dreamy everglade eyes. She sighed, stopping herself from putting her hand on his arm. "Me and a uh 'special' friend would go to Starlight."

"Starlight?" he asked.

"Yea it's this drive in theatre that's been around forever."

He rubbed his bare chin. "I used to go to drive ins as a kid, too. We would pile in my dad's truck, bring blankets and pillows. It was sweet. Am I enough of a 'special friend' to go with you?"

She pursed her lips, trying to hide her giddy smile. "Mmhm, let me change clothes." She quickly changed into a grey Spelman crewneck, with black leggings. Her braided pigtails, bouncing behind her.

When she walked towards him, Denver looked up at her with that fucking melting smile again putting his phone back in his pocket. "Ready? There's a showing in 45 minutes and we can make it." She nodded as they walked out of her door. "Don't forget to lock up and everything."

"Mmhm you don't have to tell me that." Then she bumped his hip as she heard the automatic lock.

They stopped by the gas station. "Want anything?" He asked.

"Nope just a water."

He clicked his teeth and winked, "I got you princess."

Before she could call him corny he closed the door. She forgot to tell him what water she wanted. She also wanted some gummy bears. Her body probably needed a vegetable, but her tongue was craving something sweet. When he returned he placed the bag in the backseat.

"So your not gonna hand me my water?"

He started the car. "Wouldn't you rather wait till we get there so you can sip it while watching the movie?" She responded with a shrug.

They pulled into the drive in and there were 5 cars in front of them. "Damn how many screens do they have?"

"I think 5 or 6. It's bigger than you think." After he paid and drove the winding road, the lot was in front of them. "Wow, it really looks the same. The bathrooms and snack bar are in that building in the middle in case you need it."

"I gotcha captain." Since they were 15 minutes early they got a parking spot in the 2nd row towards the right side."

"You don't want to park by people?"

He shook his head, then held up a blunt. "Nah there were people with their kids."

"Great call." Then a shiver passed over her.

Denver looked at her with concern in his eyes. "You okay?"

"Yea just cold." He reached in the backseat and Casey was hit with his sweet musky scent. It was kinda woodsy like pine, earthy but lasting. She hummed to herself as he draped a fluffy blanket over her.

"Your cum isn't on this blanket is it? Because trusting a random blanket in the backseat makes me ask."

He chuckled, "No my cum, and nobody elses is on this blanket. I keep one in the car when the temperature change. And this is a rental. You never know." She snuggled closer to it, when he looked away she smelled it. *Omg it smells like him.* She took another deeper inhale.

"If you're not careful, some of the fuzz with creep up your nostrils." Then she shoved him. When he reached back again, he got the bag from the gas station. "So you didn't tell me what you wanted, so I just assumed you liked Dasani."

He face dropped, nobody liked them.

"Kidding!" He took out a 5ooz bottle of *Essentia* water.

"This is my favorite! What made you get this one?"

He looked away, "Oh I might have noticed the stack of them in your pantry while I was cooking. Great brand choice by the way." He continued digging in the bag and pulled out, sour gummy worms, a veggie medley of celery and carrots, a pack of Oreos and gummy bears. Casey squealed and grabbed the veggie medley and gummy bears.

"Oh hell fucking yea." She murmured opening the pack.

He half smiled at her as she grabbed his soda and the rest of the snacks. "You have chosen wisely young one."

"Young one?" Her mouth full of bears. "I'm older than you."

Now he looked at her crazy. "No you're not. You just turned 26."

"So how old you are you? 40?"

"Nah, 28. My birthday just passed."

Surprise filled her face, "Oh? When was it?"

"You'll feel like a dick if I tell you. You never asked, so I never told." She gave him an expecting glance with an open hand. The sun was finally behind the trees and screen. "Yesterday."

Record scratch.

"Yesterday? Were birthday twins and you didn't want to tell me?"

He was quiet, "I didn't want to spoil your birthday worried about me. I guess I should've made you worry a little." She not only stood him up, but she stood him up on his birthday. Then she recalled their conversations about being dedicated to each other the night of her party and ripping each others clothes off.

"I'm sorry," she whispered.

He gently grabbed her hand, rubbing the top of his thumb above her knuckles. "You didn't know. I should've told you." Without stopping herself, she kissed his hand as an uneasy feeling stirred in her stomach. "Don't feel bad on our friend hangout, okay?"

She lowered her chin and lifted it again. The gummy bears didn't taste nearly as sweet anymore. "I'll try."

Then the movie started, he changed the radio station to the designated channel and they watched the screen as he lit the blunt. Even though it was another "Bad Boys" movie, Casey loved it. The action, the angles. She was cheering right along with Denver at the end.

When they made it back to her condo, she still thought about her selfish choice. He was in the shower now, preparing for this last night in Atlanta with her. She looked down at her hands, she was still holding his blanket. She smelled it again and thought of the perfect gift.

They cuddled in bed, facing each other. Their noses brushing against each other as his hands danced on her legs. "The night isn't over yet," he whispered.

"I know," she lightly kissed him as she scooted her breast closer to his chest. His muscles greeting her, expecting her.

"Can I tell you a secret?" She kissed his cheek.

"This is the best time for secrets," he traced his hands to the small of her back.

"I'm going to miss you."

"I'm gonna miss you too Case."

He kissed her deeply taking her by surprise, holding onto her like she would run away again if he didn't. She held onto him the same.

Please don't leave, stay with me.

She took off his boxers as he took off her panties. *This feels so good I don't want it to end,* as she rolled onto of him. His hardness pressing into her, filling her need.

When the morning light woke her up, he was gone. She rubbed her forehead with one hand on her hip. Fuck. Then she massaged her chest, the wave of guilt and disrespect returning to her.

Why did he still talk to her? Why didn't he tell her they shared a birthday?

MONDAY AFTERNOON, Casey walked into her favorite coffee shop and took a deep breath. She found this shop on Instagram and loved it. It was black owned, had good music and an incent burning. Yep these were her people. After she ordered her drip coffee with almond milk, she sat down at a table by the window. She looked through her oversized Coach tote and pulled out her laptop and opened her business launch plan.

She had the building, the poles installed and it was finally clean. Positive traction has happened. Even though she only had one day a week dedicated to her business, she was going to make it count. That's why she decided to visit this coffee shop after dusting the studio.

Suddenly, her mind went blank.

What else did she need to add to the list? She knew how to teach, and had different routines planned already. But the business management piece she needed more help with. She had never seen a pole training position or even spoken to someone who owns a pole studio. What was the best way to advertise to get to her target market?

Then an email notification appeared on her computer. Grad school applications were closing soon.

She put her head in her hands. Another degree would help in the long run, but did she have to do it right now? Why did she even want another degree? Dancing was always her passion, but she wanted to lead her own business. Coraline could just hire another trainer, even if was temporary, to replace her.

The chair next to her made a noise, she turned her head and found herself face to face with Sky. Sky smiled widely, "Hey girl! I didn't know you liked to come here."

Casey smiled and stood up to hug her, " Sky! Yes I love it here, the playlist is awesome. I would go to the library but I'm not in the mood for quiet." Sky was one of the performers at Green Envy but they were still friends. Casey trained Sky and loved her immediately.

Sky nodded, "Makes sense. What are you working on?"

"I'm opening my own pole fitness studio here. I want to teach classes, some women empowerment, host parties."

Sky's eyebrows raised, "That's a neat idea! Maybe if anyone wants to make extra cash, they can work at the club if they want. It's not shady like some others I've worked in. The fees are actually fair."

"Yea that's what I told my mom before she left as CEO. It's just trying to build the blocks to get there. I want to open around April but I'm scared to set a date. There's so much that I need and I'm so scared it won't go well. I don't know, what I don't know."

Sky twisted her lips. "Well what kind of classes would you teach? Are you going to be the only teacher? That sounds like it would be a lot for you."

She sighed and brushed her hand across her lips. "I would definitely want beginners, intermediate and professional level classes. Maybe even some pole conditioning classes, if people just want to work out."

Sky nodded, "Mmhm. I'd also add classes on floorwork and lap dances in the future. They are not the easiest moves, but it can work. Did you want to lean into sexual empowerment too? Maybe host couple events for people to dance on their partners."

A big light bulb went off in Casey's head. "Oh my God,

you're a genius Sky!" She knew she could trust her. "Do you want to teach some classes?"

Sky face stretched into a wide smile. "Sure! You know I keep some jobs. As long as I can still work at the club a few nights to make ends meet, definitely. Would I be teaching for free?"

Casey pressed her lips together, "No. I don't know what the salary would be because I haven't really gotten that far yet." This was going to take a lot more effort than she thought.

"Well, I'm still good to help and teach either way. Even if it's voluntary. Just take one step at a time. Everything will come together I promise."

Casey looked out the window, "I can't afford for it not too, honestly."

As much as she loved Grant Enterprises, she craved being on her own. Yes, her mother paid for the studio. But in order to keep it, she had to bring in revenue.

No more money, meant closing the doors that haven't even opened yet.

She leaned into her laptop and started a new list titled

'TO DO BEFORE SETTING LAUNCH DATE.'

1. Come up with a nice pussytastic perfect name

2. Advertise/make flyers coming soon (until a date is set ugh)

3. Post more pole work videos from the studio

4. Make the studio feel as safe and comfy for everyone of all backgrounds

5. Get more instructors

6. Brainstorm event ideas to bring people in

CHAPTER 11

CASEY PULLED into the address Gemini sent her for the painting studio. She circled the building twice because she couldn't change lanes fast enough. *I should've Ubered, I fucking hate driving.* A painting studio? Casey thought they were doing brunch. When she walked in, there were aprons hanging on hooks on one side of the room. On the other, a spread of brunch food like pancakes, bacon, muffins and more. Then a mimosa table with the option to make an orange juice or cranberry mimosa.

Gemini waved at her from the front row, an empty seat next to her in front of a blank canvas. Casey smiled and walked toward her.

"Hey! You made it just in time," Gemini said with a smile as they hugged. "Go fix your plate first then come back. It's all bottomless so drink and eat as much as you want."

Casey pursed her lips, "Okay! Let me fix a plate then." She made a plate of fruit, a croissant and a mainly champagne cranberry mimosa then returned to her seat. "Is this a paint and sip?"

Gemini slyly smiled, "It is. But it's not your 'average' paint event." Casey looked around the room and noticed that it was mainly ladies in the class with wide grins. What did they know that she didn't?

Suddenly, a dark chocolate man ripped in muscles wrapped in nothing but a shallow towel walked onto the platform at the front of the room. If he had fur wrapped around his shoulders, he would look like *M'baku* from Black Panther. It was quiet as his hands slowly fisted the towel and let it fall on the floor.

He wasn't wearing anything underneath.

His thick long dick was erect and out for everyone to see. His toned brown legs so cut that she had to stop herself from staring at his thighs.

"Oh," Casey whispered.

Gemini grabbed her paint brush biting her bottom lip, "Mmhm girl. That is a fine ass man. Let the inspiration come to you and onto you."

Casey whipped her neck and stuck her tongue out. "You are literally engaged to my brother Gem. Why are we in the front row?"

She shrugged back, "When you're married, you don't suddenly turn blind. I got these tickets months ago, he's a sensual influencer. He does these around the country. I snagged two tickets and I didn't want to invite Calvin. That's my man, but I also wanted to hang out with my girl." She tapped Casey's shoulder.

Casey delicately took a sip of her drink as she observed the sexy model. The curves around his shoulders, the glow of his dark skin, his full black beard.

She'd never painted, but he was beautiful enough for a canvas. So, she grabbed her brush and began to paint.

He stayed still as the other women in the room whistled

every now and then which made him grin or pet his beard. Then return back to his resting handsome face.

"So what happened with that guy from your birthday? You promised some tea would be spilled."

Casey took a bite of fruit, "Sorry. This long ass dick is sitting *right* in front of me is a serious distraction." The model chuckled but remained still.

"I don't blame you," Gemini eyed the man again from his chiseled calf up to his eyes. "He is fine fine. Now spill, because Denver seemed swooned over you so I was surprised to see you sitting AND leaving with someone else."

Casey pressed her lips together, "So I've known Ayden literally over a decade. He was my first fucking kiss. I thought he was in jail, but turns out he's a pharmacist now making big money. He left Atlanta and moved to Raleigh, North Carolina. We fucked and then I went back to my place after. Denver was mad, but I never said we were exclusive. I enjoy multiple different relationships. We don't have to talk everyday but we can have fun.

"Anyway, Denver was mad at me for ditching him. Which I get was an asshole move. But I still can be with who I want in whatever capacity I see fit. I mean the pole studio opening is coming, I'm still working with Grant Enterprises. There is a lot on my plate right now. At the end of the day, I wish I could share a bed with them both. But that's a fantasy. I doubt they would get along."

Gemini slowly dipped her brush in the paint. "Have you asked?"

Casey's face twisted, "Asked? Asked what?"

"For a threesome, with Denver and Ayden?"

She thought about it. She never asked him outright if he was open to that. "Actually no. I always thought it would be a hard no. From both of them. You've seen how Denver looks at me. I could ask him to get on his knees on a bed of nails and he'd do it in a heartbeat. A on the other hand, would not."

"The squeaky wheel gets the oil, sis. You don't get what you want without asking or demanding it."

"Have you asked for one before?" Casey asked.

Gemini gave her a look and nodded. "I actually have and do not regret the experience. I'm not sharing the details though." A reflective smile spread across Gemini's face.

She rolled her eyes. "You're a freak you know that right?"

"I invited you to an erotic paint and sip, Casey. I'm very much a freak." They laughed and raised their glasses to each other. "You should look into poly though. I think it sounds like your ally."

"Poly? Like have multiple husbands?"

"No," Gemini chuckled. "That's polygamy. I'm talking about solo polyamory. It's basically when you're single, but have multiple different relationships that have different meaning. That's a simple breakdown, but you should look into it."

"Oh you want me to be one of those bitches with hella men on their arm."

Gemini pretended to look around the room and leaned in, "Is that not everyones dream? I mean you still need personal time without them. But, nothing wrong with some good fun."

Casey rolled her eyes, "Mmm true. Anyways, enough about me. How has wedding planning been going?"

Her face fell. "At this point, I want to go to a courthouse. The date is months away but I'm so anxious. I can't decide on the color scheme and the wedding planner is getting on my last nerve about it. I've barely put the wedding party together. I only want one maid of honor, Calvin has one best man. But we still need a flower girl. I don't know any kids, and I'm NOT inviting anyone from work."

Casey thought about it, "My girl Sky has a little girl named

Nettie. She's 4 or 5. Definitely adorable enough to be a flower girl."

Gemini's eyes lit up, "Can you ask Sky if that's okay? I don't know her but I'd really appreciate it. She'd have an invite of course."

"I got you." A painter cleared her throat behind Casey. "I think the room wants us to shut up now."

They smiled and looked back at the painting, then the model and winked at them. Casey's painting could generally tell it was a man. But she didn't paint the dick because, she didn't want a random dick on her walls at home.

The organizer of the event stepped onto the stage in a maxi dress and sandals. "Thank you everyone for coming! Please follow our model on your socials to stay up to date with his events."

He confidently stood up, and said in a deep invigorating voice "Thank you ladies it's been a pleasure." The entire room swooned.

Casey wondered what *he* was doing later. She hugged and squeezed Gemini, carefully grabbed her painting and went home. After she hung the painting on the wall in her bedroom, she took a picture for social media with the caption *beauty is in the eye of the non-painter*.

For dinner, she decided that spaghetti and garlic bread were the best options since it could be made quickly and efficiently. When she pulled the spaghetti out of the oven her phone was ringing. Denver was facetiming her. She stuck her tongue out and answered. "Hey Case," she said with a cool smile.

"Hey cutie, how was your day?"

He was sitting in his place in the living room. His phone was propped on his coffee table. "It was good. I cleaned my house, talked to my mom for a little bit. I'd say it was productive. What about you?"

"Pretty good, I just finished cooking dinner and I painted a dick today."

Denver coughed loudly and sat up. "You what? Painted a dick? Did you just walk up to a man and paint his dick? I'm confused."

She roared with laugher, "The look on your face is priceless! But no, Gemini took me to a sensual paint and sip."

"A sensual paint and sip where you painted a dick? I'm still lost."

"A model posed while we painted his dick."

He nodded with his chin in his hand looking at her. "Uh huh. May I see this dick painting?"

She got up, went into her room and flipped the camera so he could see the painting.

"Okay, I see now. It's kind of like an abstract painting of a man sitting in a chair. You didn't even paint the dick though."

"Well I don't want to stare at another man's dick all the time."

They laughed together and he got a swoon look in his eye again. "Can I take your picture? I'd rather ask permission than you randomly see 'Denver took a facetime photo of you' 17 times."

She rolled her eyes trying to hide her blush, "Sure." She smiled and he took a few photos, the flash coming across her screen a few times. She even stuck her tongue out for one. When she thought he was done, she looked away and he took another. "Alright, now it's my turn. You know I'm a professional so you need to stand up and open your curtain."

"No problem." Denver got up from the couch and opened his curtain. The sunlight gleaming from his eyes like a gemstone. His freckles gathered on this tip of his nose and cheeks.

She took photos gassing him up. "Look at you with your cute light skinned self. Give me a smile!" He laughed as she took more photos. Then he stuck his tongue out like her. "You want to be me so bad. Copy cat!"

"I want to be inside you baby." The weight in his voice made Casey stand still. "I miss you."

"I miss you too. When are you coming down here again? Even though you were just here."

Denver brushed his knuckles against his jaw, "I actually wanted to ask if you'd fly out to Nashville."

"Nashville? Why Nashville?"

"Would you want to spend Christmas with the Hayes family? My family. I'd love to see you again and show you were I grew up."

She was speechless. "Christmas? Like the holiday?"

"Yes your not a Jehovah's witness are you? You are aware of the gift giving pagan holiday where people sit around a Christmas tree, right? There is music, carols, Jesus being born."

"Yes obviously. It just threw me off. Why do you want me to meet your family?"

He took a deep breath. "I know your not my girlfriend, but your really special to me. I'd really like to see you again and have you enjoy my family. I think you'd have fun on the ranch. There are horses and my mom has a beautiful greenhouse. A nice vacation with nice people, that's all, as friends."

"You aren't going to try a Christmas proposal are you?"

He laughed, "No I promise. I learned my lesson the first time."

"Let me talk to my mom first. I've never spent a Christmas away from home. When do I need to let you know?"

"At least within the next three days so I can get our plane tickets."

"Okay let me give my mom a call then and I'll let you know."

A silly grin filled his face, "Awesome. Well I'll let you go so you can eat dinner. I'll talk to you later baby."

"Talk to you later babe." She blew a kiss at the end of the call. He took a photo at the last minute.

CASEY USED her key to open the front door of the mansion. "Mommy, I'm here!" She called.

"I'm in the kitchen!" She answered back, rocking her hips to Whitney Houston.

Casey squeezed and rocked her mom in the pantry. "My baby, what's new!"

"Oh um, let's not talk about me yet. What's new with you? What do you fill your time with since being retired?"

"Oh. I have a schedule. Swimming on Tuesday and Thursday followed by a massage, Zumba class Mondays and Fridays, and something random on Saturday. Sunday's are for the family," She pinched Casey's cheek. She knew she was Mom's favorite, but she wasn't going to tell anyone.

"Wow that is a busy schedule mom. I see why you needed that nap the other day."

Mama pulled what she needed from the cabinet, "I didn't need the nap, dear. It simply called out to me and I answered." They laughed as they moved to sit in the living room. "Now, what's going on with you?"

"Well I know Thanksgiving is next week, and I'll be here for that of course. But a friend of mine invited me to spend Christmas with his family."

Mama froze. "With his family?"

She did a nervous smile, "Yep."

"Where does his family live?"

Casey pressed her lips together, "Tennessee."

"Tennessee?" Mama questioned.

"Mmhm Christmas in Nashville, Tennessee."

"Well, he must be special if your agreeing to go to and spend the first holiday away from your family. Even when you were in school, you came home for the holidays." She gave Casey a questioning look.

"I know mom. But my gut is telling me to go and he's just a friend."

"Yea you can keep telling yourself that. Help me finalize the Thanksgiving menu, I need you to go to the store to pick up a few things."

Casey hugged her mom as they stood up and went back into the kitchen.

With them texting everyday, she sent him weekly photos of her posing in the studio, cleaning and she and Calvin repainting the parking lot lines.

No matter the photo, Denver always responded the most ridiculous way.

If you send another photo of you sweating in the sun I might faint.

I love the way your bottom lip pouts in the 2nd picture. I can't wait to kiss them again.

Are those pink knee high socks? You're making your man go crazy states away.

WHILE CASEY WAS DOING her night time skin care routine in her vanity mirror, Denver was on FaceTime admiring her and the products. Then started pretending he was doing a voice over.

"And now she's put on an eye patch? An under eye patch? I don't know what it does but it makes her look great. Even though she doesn't need it. And now, you know the bottle Fenty! Is that moisturizer?"

Casey laughed as she rubbed into her skin, "Shut up. So you really want to spend Christmas with me? Even though we are not dating."

He rolled his eyes, "Yes I would like for you to spend Christmas with me as a *friend*. Either way, I'd like to introduce you to my parents as a, *friend*. I honestly miss you, a lot."

She blushed, it's been weeks and the anticipation of seeing him next month was becoming real. It was nice that he missed her too. "I miss you, too. I'm kind of excited. What is your family like around the holidays?"

Denver chuckled, "Very eccentric. They have had their decoration ups since October. We also have family traditions. So be ready to be festive."

Casey's eyes widened. "How festive are we talking?"

"Matching pajamas festive."

"Well don't put me on the Christmas card unless I approve it, got it?"

They laughed together, "Got it. What about your family?"

"Well thanksgiving is more crowded than Christmas because that's when my dad's side will join us. I'm not really looking forward to it." She shrugged. "You can't pick family."

"That's the truth. I grew up getting 'looks' from my dad's side."

Casey started putting her products away and clearing the

table. "What's the saddest movie in your opinion? Like every time you watch it, your crying."

He took a deep breath and looked off camera as his head lifted along with his body. "*Schindler's List*. I cry so much during that movie. The way it ends, the amount of people and generations impacted." He coughed, "I break down. What about you?"

"*Boyz N the Hood*. A great movie, but when they lay Ricky on the couch. I'm in pieces. Everyone worked their part."

Denver groaned, "Yes, John Singleton did an amazing job with that movie. That's definitely top three of the rawest death scenes in a movie. I get chocked up when Ricky's Mom opens the test scores. Like damn. That drove the nail in. Don't get me started about *Do The Right Thing*."

"Yooo I boohoo cried the first time I saw it. Calvin and I were literally crying and shaking. Meanwhile Coraline was just... frozen. That's a movie that sparks conversation, but I can't go there right now or I will start crying."

Denver nodded in agreement. "We can change the subject.

"What's your favorite drink?" Casey asked gazing at herself in the mirror.

"Well being a man from Tennessee, it's definitely whiskey. Especially Uncle Nearest."

Her face twisted, "Nearest what?"

"No it's called Uncle Nearest. He literally taught Jack Daniel everything he knew. Nearest Green was a slave that got hired by Jack to run his distillery. But out of the two, everyone know Jack Daniel's and not Uncle Nearest. It's my favorite because it's historical and it tastes better."

Her eyebrow raised. "Woah I had no idea it was that deep. I'll have to try it one day."

"Yea maybe one day you can visit me and see how I live?"

Casey scoffed. "I don't fly out to visit people. I fly for work and call who's there."

Denver looked taken aback. "Damn, got it. Well good night."

"Good ni-." The call ended.

Even though Casey shrugged as she stood up from her fluffy seat, a wave of guilt filled her stomach. She did throw that comment in his face. *Let's be mature.* She texted him.

Me: Sorry that came out that way. I didn't mean to sound like that

Denver: ....

Denver: I get it. I know my place. GN

CHAPTER 12

AS CASEY WAS DRIVING to her mom's house for Thanksgiving dinner, she was still spit balling business names. Pink pole? Nope. Floating fun Pole studio? Nah. Shake your tail pole emporium? Just awful. She hated everything she came up with so far.

Thanksgiving was filled with random family members and good ass food. You could watch a parade, eat good and have food for the rest of the week and not have to buy gifts. Ham was good on Christmas, but it taste better at Thanksgiving. She decided a long sleeve orange ribbed dress was best for the occasions. All of Casey's family came over, even the aunt that always asked 'when are you having kids? Where is your man?' She would always scoff and roll her eyes. Aunt Paulette was Bull's sister, her biological sperm doner. Her and Mama grew up best friends so when she started dating her brother, it became a trio.

Auntie's long red nails securely held her Solo cup, gold and emerald rings covered almost each finger. "Ya Mama told me you won't be home for Christmas."

"Hey Auntie," She tried to not say sarcastically. "Yea my friends and I rented a cabin in Nashville. Mama told you?"

"Duh. She's been telling me everything since before you or any of your siblings were a thought in ya mama's eye. I remember when your mama didn't have shit but the pole and the walls of y'all place. Fuck I stayed there too for a minute. That's where yo mama and daddy met. Your mama couldn't keep a secret from me if she tried. That's sis for life."

Casey tried to side eye to herself. "Yea, I've heard the story." Auntie still loves her brother. She knew how Casey felt about him. But she still continued.

"Is a boy gonna be there?"

That didn't last long. "I really don't think that's your business. I thought you knew everything." Casey filled her cup with ice from the fridge dispenser.

Aunt Pauline scoffed. "I wish yo daddy coulda made it. I still visit him every Tuesday. The niggas been doing good. When was the last you made the time to see him? The other reason y'all got all this shit is because of him. But he doesn't get to enjoy it, huh."

"No, but you do Auntie. You still make sure to 'sweep by' during the holidays."

Coraline swiftly came around the corner, "Oh Casey! I just remembered there's something I need your help with in the pantry." She grabbed and pulled her elbow so fast that neither her or Auntie Pauline could fit more words in. They quickly went into the pantry and Coraline closed the door behind them, her hand on her hip.

"Why are you over there talking to that bitter ass lady? You know you don't talk to her."

Casey stomped as she paced the pantry, trying to ignore the mix match containers. Not in my house. "She's so annoying bruh. Why is she acting like that man didn't kill multiple people AND have a fucking 9 year old pushing coke. Coke! But I'm being an asshole for not seeing him?"

Coraline put her hands in front of her, "First, I need you to take a deep breath." Casey made a deadpan face as she breathed through her nose.

"There."

"Now we still have dinner that's about to start. Are you going to be able to not leap across the table? Not saying Pauline doesn't deserve it, but Mama definitely doesn't deserve the embarrassment".

She frowned, "Yea fine."

Calvin snuck into the pantry, surprised to find his sisters. "What are y'all doing in here?"

"Avoiding Pauline." Casey said.

Calvin nodded. "No need to say anything more." He reached behind a container and pulled out a book. They looked at him confused.

"I always keep a book in here. This is a soundproof hiding spot in the house, kind of relaxing."

They rolled his eyes. "You're lame as hell," Coraline said with a chuckle.

The door opened again and Gemini stepped in. "Wow it's more cramped in here than I thought. Mama sent me to get you all. Dinner is about to start."

They sat at the table, like a good family. Mama spent the rest of the dinner trying to get the sweet potato pie recipe from Aunt Lorraine. Casey was thankful to be around so many people during the holidays. Then seeing how he lit up when Gemini sat next to him, holding his hand, filled her heart more. She would miss them on Christmas. Even though they weren't the 'matching pajama' type, it was still a family occasion.

She couldn't imagine her sperm donor at the table, even if

he's a big reason why they have the table and the home they are enjoying.

～

CASEY WALKED into the coffee shop again. Despite the fact that they closed earlier between the weeks of Thanksgiving and Christmas, she couldn't miss out. "Case!"

She turned toward to voice to see Sky in a hoodie with a laptop on her table, while her daughter, Nettie sat in the chair next to her extravagantly coloring and quiet.

"Hey y'all, hey Nettie!"

She looked up with her big brown eyes, took her thumb out her mouth, waved and returned to drawing. Nettie was close to 5 now. When Casey first met her she was 2 years old, running around the lockers. To see her quiet and drawing was vastly different from her opening backpacks for fun backstage or jumping out of lockers to scare anyone who walked past. Sky stood up and hugged her. "Wassup! Do you want anything? I just ordered a blueberry muffin for Nettie. It should be out any minute."

Casey waved her down, "No no, it's fine. Lemme put my jacket and purse down then get some chicken noodle soup."

She placed her order and brought a hot muffin to the table. The server brought the soup to Casey a few minutes later. Nettie's missing tooth showed as she made a OOM sound biting into the soft bread. "Mmm mmm. Fanks Mommy for the buffin."

"Your welcome boo, don't talk with your mouth full." Sky grabbed a napkin from the table and wiped crumbs off Nettie's chin. "Okay so I had a few questions that I wanted to ask. If I'm prying then don't answer."

Casey nodded as she blew the steam off the soup. "Please

you may be saving my life with the question. I don't know what the fuck is going on."

Sky cleared her throat and glanced at Nettie.

"Sorry. I don't know what's going on. I do know I need to be open and functioning as soon as possible."

Sky nodded leaning into her laptop, casually glancing over at Nettie. "First, where is the studio?"

She swallowed. "It's kind of past Krog Street Market. The street it's on has alot foot traffic."

She scrunched her face and looked away.

"What does that mean? Why that face? It's close to the Beltline so great business opportunity right? It kinda gives warehouse vibes but it's clean. You can see the people walk by and everything. I got curtains."

"I don't think the studio should be on a foot traffic heavy place. You know we mainly wear sports bras and shorts, sometimes underwear. You know the more skin, the better stick to the pole. I don't want creeps with their hands in their 'pocket' watching us."

Casey's eyes widened. "Fu-, I mean wow I haven't even thought about that."

"I'm glad I said something. Also, what's the name of the studio?"

"I've been beating my head on a name for weeks."

"You need a name before a business license. I'm assuming you don't have that either."

"Nope. I didn't even realize I needed that."

"Well when will it be open? What hours would you have classes and what days?"

She shrugged again. "I was going to wait until I hired the instructors first before figuring out a class schedule."

Sky's face twisted with lifted eyebrows again.

"Stop doing that!"

She put her hands up, "I'm just saying they may ask that question when your interviewing them. It's better to work out at least a schedule idea that works for you and them. How about we work on it together hmm?" Just as they leaned into Sky's laptop, Nettie pulled on Casey's long sleeve.

"Cuse me miss Casey. But um uh can you get me another muffin?"

Sky cut her eye, "You haven't even finished this one Net."

"BUT MAMA IT'S COLD NOW!" Nettie screamed.

Sky sighed wiping her eyebrow. "How about I ask if they can reheat it for you mmm?" Nettie gap showed again as she smiled. "But I won't ask if you scream again."

Nettie kicked her feet excitedly and nodded as Sky stood up with the plate in her hand. "I'll be right back."

As Sky was at the front desk passing the plate, Nettie began coloring again. "I seen a roach at home. It was really really big. Mommy's friend killed it though. They make funny noises when I watch TV."

Casey tried to act like she wasn't shocked. "Oh really?"

Nettie nodded kicking her feet more. "Ya ya when I knock on Mommy's door she says I can't come in. So I just go back to watching TV. Do you got *Bluey* on yo phone?"

Casey shakes her head. "No I don't."

"It's on mommy's phone. Want to play it with me?"

"Sure, maybe the next time I come over since I'm talking to Mommy."

"Kay." Then she returned to her coloring book.

Sky was walking back to the table with a new plate and a new muffin cut in half. "Sorry they wouldn't reheat the old muffin so I bought half of a new one."

"Mommy I'm full I don't want a muffin no more. My tummy is full Mommy." Sky gave Casey a deadpan stare.

"That's fine baby."

Then Casey and Sky started building a 5 day schedule being open from 3pm to 7pm Wednesday through Sunday. Sky emailed the spreadsheet to Casey, she squeezed her in thanks. "How did you even think about that Sky?"

"If there is anything I've had to learn how to do, is schedule for Nettie's sake. My work schedule, her school schedule, daycare, holidays." She exhaled. "If I'm not thinking 3 months, 6 months and 2 years ahead then Nettie falls behind and I won't have that."

They all stood up from the table. Nettie asked Casey to zip up her jacket and she did while making a funny noise. Nettie giggled and did a little dance.

While Sky was putting everything back in her bag, she asked Casey. "Want to go to the park with me after the holidays? We can meet up again, share more ideas. I'd love to see the studio when you come back from your trip."

Oh yea, the trip to Nashville with Denver. "I'd love to."

CHAPTER 13

DENVER AND CASEY arranged their flights to land two days before Christmas in Nashville at the same time. The airport was crowded from everyone traveling for the holidays, a sea of reds and greens surrounded them as they passed construction equipment after leaving baggage claim. Denver carried their luggage as they bobbed and weaved. Was he upset carrying the pink duffle bag? Not at all because the beautiful woman next to him was wearing a pink Victoria's Secret sweat set with white UGGs.

When they stepped outside, Casey shivered, "Damn is the air always this cold?"

He nodded wrapping his arm around her shoulders. "No it is hot in the summer." He rubbed her arm as a red F150 pulled in front of them. Casey was about to run but the white man jumped out and hugged Denver kissing his head.

"Brian! My boy how ya doin?"

"I'm good dad what about you?"

"Bout damn killed myself putting up the lights for your

mama. But I survived another year. Is this the beautiful young lady?"

She smiled as Denver introduced her. "Dad this is my... friend Casey. Casey this is my dad."

She extended her hand, "Nice to meet you."

"Oh come over here we hug." She made a face at Denver as she accepted the loving bear hug. "Mom already made dinner but yall can get settled in first." Mr. Hayes put their luggage in the back and Denver helped her into the truck.

As Denver and his dad caught up for the 30 minutes ride, they pulled up to a set of large black metal gates. Mr. Hayes typed in a code and the gates swung open to a long drive way that led to a large three story mansion. Casey couldn't even see where their property ended.

"Welcome to our home," Mr. Hayes said with a twang.

The roof was dark brown with multiple A-frames. The home had large windows with a sunroom. There was a covered carport and another garage behind it. Then the yard got her attention. There were three blow up Santa's, lit up reindeers, a sleigh and a snowman. The trim of the house was wrapped in garland from what she could see from the headlights.

"Your home is so beautiful and festive."

Mr. Hayes grinned, "Why thank you sweetheart! We put the garland up every year. You'll see the house better in the day."

When they walked in the front door and hung up their jackets, Mrs. Hayes came around the corner. Her chestnut skin glowing with her silk pressed silver hair in a clip at the back. "Is this sweet Casey? We've heard so much about you! Welcome and Merry Christmas!"

She hugged them tightly and kissed Denver on the cheek. "My boy is home for Christmas. We made up the guest bedroom upstairs."

"The guest bedroom, as in were sharing?"

"No need to be shy with us," Mrs. Hayes says with a wink. "Just be mindful of your volume. We're down the hall to the left, in the master suite but just in case."

Casey's face filled with heat, unsure of what to say. "Uh thank you so much Mrs. Hayes. I'm excited for my first Hayes' Christmas."

A wide grin spread on her face, "We're excited to have you as our guest. You'll find a little somethin on y'all's bed."

Once upstairs, Denver placed her bags in front of the closet. The king-size bed had a snowflake quilt on the comforter. The window showed the manicured backyard with a pergola and sitting area around a fire pit. Then she saw the cracked open door to the left which was a large en suite bathroom with a standing shower, two sinks and water closet. There was a wreath decorated in red ribbons and pine cones on the wall next to the mirrors. On the sink were two sets of towels, cloths, and holiday-themed foaming hand soap.

When Casey stepped out of the bathroom, she looked back at the bed. Forest green robs, matching flannel pajamas, with their initials stitched on the left side. *CG.* Maybe one day hers would say C.H. *Chill out don't let the Christmas magic get you.*

"Wow, robes and pajamas?"

Denver smiled wider holding his up in adoration. "She did these herself, I can tell from this gold thread. My mom really enjoys hosting. I'll bring up my stuff, you go ahead and get comfortable." He came back with his things and began placing them in the dresser drawers.

"Need me to unpack your bag?"

"No I'm fine. I usually just live out of my suitcase wherever I'm at."

He arched his eyebrow. "Really?"

"Yea unless if I'm there a month or longer."

"I gotcha." They heard a light knock on the door. After they were acknowledged Mr. Hayes' head came through. "Hey kiddos. Come downstairs for dinner when your ready."

"Thank you!" Casey said excited. "I'll be down after we freshen up."

"Of course hun, see yall in a bit."

Denver went into the bathroom taking off his shirt. The muscles standing out on his caramel skin. "Psst."

She turned towards the bathroom door to him peeking out.

"What?" She whispered back.

He waved, motioning for her, "Come here."

She shook her head. "No," she said quickly. "Your parents are literally downstairs. Like right below us right now."

He shrugged. "Just don't sneak up on them. I learned that lesson the hard way." She looked at their door and back at him, he lifted his pecks twice. "3..2..."

"Alright fine I'll come in." She rolled her eyes and stepped into the bathroom. What she didn't see behind the door was that Denver was already naked. Very naked "Ooo okay."

Then he pulled a mistletoe from behind his back and hung it above her head. Then he cleared his throat with puckered lips.

"Fine," she murmured with a smile as their lips met. First it was light, then Denver leaned in deeper to her, pulling her closer than she already was. "How about we turn on the shower?" He sucked on her bottom lip as he leaned back and turned on the shower.

THEY FIGURED by the time they actually made it downstairs his parents would be in bed. He was right. The spaghetti was still in the pot so they quickly fixed their bowls. When Casey took her first bite, her eyes were closed. "Mmm this is so good. There's an ingredient in here I'm trying to name. Is it rosemary? Mint?"

He nodded taking his already umpteenth bite. "Mmhm."

"From how your tearing up your plate, I'm assuming this is exactly what you wanted."

"Hell yea," he wiped his mouth and continued eating. "I would always ask for this as a kid and even now. I will never turn down from spaghetti, especially my moms."

Her heart warmed, thinking about the times her, her mom and Coraline would work together in the kitchen.

After they finished eating, they washed their dishes and placed them in the dishwasher. Casey wanted to sit outside, but when she opened the sliding back door the cool air hit her. Denver was next to her immediately with blankets, marshmallows and metal skewers.

"What are those for?"

He shrugged. "I was about to roast some marshmallows and make s'mores. Would you like to join me?"

She took a blanket. "Sure, even if it is balls cold outside. S'mores are kind of corny though."

He slid open the door for her after the heavy blanket was around her shoulder. "You're in the Hayes household. Cheesy and corny is all we do at Christmas time." He chuckled. "Just wait until Christmas Eve."

"Oh gosh. That's why you wanted me to come? The Christmas magic isn't going to work on me." She sat down in front of the fire pit as he put the fire in.

"Christmas magic? We just make s'mores when it's cold out," he said innocently, while smiling.

She pressed her lips together, "Uh huh."

As they sat outside, Casey took in the views of the large

hills and the mountains behind them. The stars seemed to be brighter than they were in Atlanta.

"You know this fire pit wasn't always here. I built this with my dad when I was a teenager. My mom wanted one SO bad. When we made it happen right before it got cold, she sat in front of it every night for a week. Just staring at the mountains, like how you are." She glanced at him and he smiled shyly looking away.

"So you're saying I look like your mom?"

"No," he made a face. "I meant that the mountains are beautiful and it's something y'all have in common."

"We've been here 10 minutes and your country accent is coming back stronger."

He shrugged. "This is my home." They sat in silence watching the fire and the hills. She didn't realize how loud the background noise really was in her condo. Constant honking, neighbors, yelling, the sound of people in general. But here it was quiet. The way the blanket hung around her shoulders in front of the fire made her relax. She only had to worry about what was happening right in front of her. Even listening to the cold wind pass made her feel more at peace.

She was happy with Denver. That was a fact.

I'm still not his girlfriend and that's okay with me.

Christmas Eve

When Casey woke up for breakfast, there was a buffet downstairs. Muffins, fresh fruit, scrambled eggs, Christmas tree shaped pancakes, French toast, bacon, sausage and orange juice. "Wow this looks so good! I'm starving."

Denver quickly descended the steps behind her. "I'll beat you!"

She laughed as she ran on her toes to the island. "Ooo mimosas?"

"Oh we are not a virgin household here honey." Mrs. Hayes chimed. "Please help yourself. There is more fruit in the fridge if you want a cranberry mimosa."

Denver was sitting at the dining table eating while she was making her plate. She grabbed a muffin, eggs, strawberries from the fridge and filled a glass with a mimosa.

Mr. Hayes was reading the newspaper. In the light he could be mistaken for the original James Bond. He put the paper down, taking a sip of water. "Casey," he sang. "Brian was telling us that you're opening a studio."

She smiled. He really did tell them about her. She also reminded herself to call Denver his government name Brian. Not the nickname she gave him. "I am. I really want to empower woman while encouraging them to move their bodies. I grew up dancing and wanted to keep doing it, but in my own way. Beauty has so many different definitions. It helps me stay fit, while also build confidence."

"Very true. I remember when hunny bunny was working to lose the baby weight and did different classes. What did you do dear?"

"Salsa, yoga, line dancing, Pilates, a little bit of break-dancing too. But don't tell anyone. I wasn't any good." They laughed together.

After breakfast, Denver gave her the home tour. The bedrooms, bathrooms, the walking trail that led to a real ranch with two horses. It was a gift Mr.Hayes gave Mrs. Hayes when she retired early. People came to take care of the horses full time. His parents would sometimes come out and ride them together around the 8 acres they owned.

They made it back in the house just in time for lunch. Mrs. Hayes made sandwiches. Denver asked for a BLT and Casey asked for a Turkey and Ham club sandwich with lettuce, tomato and mayo. They ate in front of the TV. The Hayes were doing a Christmas special marathon for the next 48 hours and Casey secretly loved it. Now they were watching "Jingle All the Way" laughing with Sinbad.

WHILE THE SUN WAS SETTING, they all sat together at the large sectional, Denver's arm was around Casey's shoulders and she scooted closer to him as they watched a "Charlie Brown Christmas" special. Everyone was wearing their matching robes cuddling. His parents were on the far side of the sectional. His dads arms around Mrs. Hayes shoulders, kissing her temple.

Casey then leaned her head right above his heart, feeling his heartbeat on her eardrums. Then she took a deep breath, breathing in his musty minty scent. Then his chest vibrated from a chuckle that made her open her eyes. He looked down at her with gleaming eyes. She couldn't read the emotion in them, but she lifted her head and kissed him. *This is why he wants to claim someone, claim me.* Someone's heartbeat to listen to, someone to hold in good times or bad. She looked over at his parents still cuddled together. She couldn't imagine seeing them everyday growing up and not eagerly waiting for your soulmate.

Suddenly an alarm went off on Mr. Hayes' phone and Mrs. Hayes' smiled so hard that there were crinkles by her eyes. "Oh Brian, please tell me you remember our dance. We have to do it, please please."

Denver rolled his eyes with a smile as he started to rise from the couch. "You are not allowed to record anything do you hear me?"

Casey arched her eyebrow as she flipped her phone face-down. Mrs. Hayes took a ready stance in the middle of the room with her hands behind her back. Denver stood next to her.

His dad came back into the room with *"Sleigh Ride"* by TLC blasting on a speaker from kitchen. Mr. Hayes came running to stand on the other side of Mrs. Hayes. Denver took a step forward with a pretend microphone in his hand as his parents did the electric slide behind him.

Oh he wasn't kidding about the corniness.

Then he flipped the robe behind him like he was singing for Casey and she cheered through her laughs. Even when he said giddy up saying each verse word for word. Then for the finally he did a spin into a split, with a bent back leg. Quickly falling into line with the electric slide, waving Casey up from the couch. She's still laughing as she joined in dancing with them, flipping up her robe when she kicked her leg up. Then Mrs. Hayes started dancing with Mr. Hayes, throwing it back as he kept beat with her.

Denver sighed loudly as he started dancing with Casey, kissing her cheek. Her face was starting to hurt from the joy and laughter. Then he dipped her, placing a long kiss on her lips while his parents cheered them on. When she was finally upright, spinning from the kiss, his dad said "You fell right in line Casey! I hope you'll be joining us again next year."

Then the smile started to fade. I'm not his girlfriend. "My mom would hate me if I missed another Christmas at home."

"No worries dear," Mrs. Hayes reassured smacking Mr. Hayes' hand.

After the performance, everyone retreated to their rooms to either scroll on phones or watch more movies. "Favorite Christmas album?" he asked as he select the next holiday movie.

"8 Days of Christmas" by Destiny's Child.

He smiled and scoffed. "So you admit, your in the Bey Hive?"

"I got the CD for Christmas one year when I was a kid and whew. I played it until it scratched. Calvin was the only one that would sit with me and listen to it. Coraline had homework, basketball practice, or whatever else. Whenever I listen to "Winter Paradise", I think about Calvin and I jumping and singing along. We could only hang out like that in my room, though."

Denver nodded as he placed his head on her chest. "I don't think I have one. But I guess Nat King Cole's. I listen to it the most this time of year." Her hand found its way in his curls, drawing small circles on his scalp. When Denver fell asleep to "Polar Express", she kissed the top of his head, then slipped out of bed. She tip toed downstairs to place their gifts under the tree and grab a midnight snack. But the kitchen light was on.

"Sorry. I didn't know anyone else was awake."

His mom smiled and waved her in. "Come in sweetie. I was just finishing the icing on this cake. Are you excited to see Santa?"

Casey chuckled, brushing her hand against the wall as she took a seat at the large butchers island. "Yea this is his busy night isn't it. Thank you again for the robe and pajamas. The robe is so comfy." She still hadn't taken it off from earlier.

Mrs. Hayes beamed as her dark tan freckled hand gracefully moved around the red velvet cake. The cream cheese icing danced on her knife as the cake spun.

Casey watched her, her chin rested on her hand. Lost in the spin and focus in her eyes. "Why did you get married?" she asked.

Mrs. Hayes smiled as she wiped icing off her hands in a reflective way. Then looked towards her bedroom door. "Because I have never met another man like my husband." she chuckled. "He's always been like this. When we dated in our 20s he always still did little things to let me know he cared. He's spoiled me with love, dancing and laughter for over 30 years. You know laughter is medicinal. A joyful heart is a light heart. My son got his love for laughter from us. My husband gave me a beautiful son and has been an excellent father figure. It took him some time, but I was patient. Love is patient and kind." She paused icing the cake.

"He's also mindful of my peace. You shouldn't be around people that negatively impact your spirit. When I wanted to buy this ranch, some of my "old" friends thought I was crazy. Brain was just born, I was on leave from work, we had so many excuses not to. But he encouraged me, even built the stable in the back for me, for my happiness. It makes me happy being here, raising my family here. Now I have the opportunity to not only live in my dream home, but pass it down to my son and his family." She waved towards the view. "We've been blessed."

Casey glanced out of the back window, the view of the stars were clear. Then she squinted, she swore something red flew in the sky. "Did you see that?" She asked.

"Mmhm," she looked at her watch. "Looks like Santa is on schedule." She placed a lid on the cake display case and winked at Casey. "Good night sweetheart, don't let the dreams of sugar plums keep you up."

Casey smiled at her then looked back out the window. *I know I saw something red.* The dark sky made the stars shine brighter.

When she got back in the bed, Denver was still asleep. His brown curls tossed around his pillow. She got in the bed and opened his arm, laying her head on his chest. He grunted then returned to snoring. "I love your family," she whispered into his skin. "They're making me fall in love with you." She said it out loud and believed it.

But just because you love someone, doesn't mean you're theirs forever.

Love was painful.

Casey had more things to worry about then falling in love. But the sound of Denver's slow breathing and feeling the rise and fall of his chest, made her want to sleep with him forever.

This was why he's so eager to start a family. He wanted this all the time. she closed her eyes and her dreams weren't of sugar plums but studio visions:

Casey was on the bar with her arm at second position. She was in a class with 30 other girls, but only one girl looked like her. "New combination! Grand plié, coupé, passé, plié revelé." The thin French teacher with cheekbones sharp enough to cut clapped with each word. Casey took a deep breath and looked at herself in the mirror. Her butt was growing. She already had to size up tights. Her feet grew two shoe sizes in 2 weeks so she was wearing new ballet shoes.

"Now turn!" The instructor shouted. "Again!"

Casey bent her knees and did a deep plié, trying to keep up with the other girls. Be stronger, be faster.

Casey turned her head and was suddenly on a stage wearing a fluffy white tutu and white leotard. Her hair was pressed, yanked and gelled into a bun. She got ready in a room with 100 other girls, but she didn't care. Her toes were broken and bloody. This was her solo. The solo she earned. The solo 10 girls missed out on.

She was a sugar plum fairy. A black sugar plum fairy. She was on pointe, turning and lifting around the stage, fairy lights in her hands. She appeared weightless as she floated around the stage, lifting her legs and arms with a light smile on her face. Then ended into a graceful deep curtsey as the crowd roared in applause.

The wonderful stage.

Christmas Day

Casey got dressed and put on the pajamas Mrs. Hayes gifted and Christmas socks with dancing reindeer. Denver watched her as she applied her concealer. Then began her lip routine. "Oo your doing the brown lip liner with the lip gross? I can't wait to kiss that off." He leaned forward and kissed her hair, scared to mess up her makeup.

"Behave," she said with a chuckle. "We can't look like all we do is fuck each other."

He rolled his eyes.

"Were friends remember?" she playfully reminded him with a sly smile.

He gave her puppy eyes, "Even on Christmas?"

She leaned back and lightly kissed his lips, "Shh. I might break the rule."

They walked down the stairs holding hands into the living room. Maybe she could pretend for the holiday. His parents were sitting under the tree, his mom sitting in his dads lap. "Merry Christmas!" they cheered together.

"Merry Christmas!" they sang back. Since Casey already placed their gifts under the tree. She got his mom a pine scented candle, that she loved. His dad a pocket knife, because she figured most men liked knives.

"You know I broke my last one Casey. This is neat thank you!"

"You're welcome, Mr. Hayes."

She didn't know what to get Denver until it hit her at the last minute at the mall in the Men's department. She handed him the wrapped box, hoping she guessed right. He seemed surprised after opening. It was a cologne with deep woodsy notes and a red sweater. After smelling it, he sprayed it on his pajamas and gave her a cheesy grin. "This is perfect Casey.

I've had my eye on this one for a few weeks. How did you know?"

She knew her nose wouldn't lead her astray. "I had a feeling."

"Now it's my turn." As long as it wasn't a ring, she was good. There were a couple large wrapped boxes behind the tree that he pushed forward.

"Oh my gosh what is it?!"

"Open it and see." He said with a smile.

A dog better not jump out of here. *I literally can't.* She quickly pulled back the wrapping paper, opening the box. It was a full set of the new collection of Fenty skin products. Her iris' would be hearts if she could see them.

"There's more in there."

"More?" Casey continued to pull out 4 matching short sets that were a variety of pink shades, a blush pink yoga mat, two pink covered romance novels, a Paris Hilton cookware set and 2 pairs of Nikes. "I think I'm going to have a stroke."

Denver and his family joined in laughter. "I couldn't decide what to get you. So I just said, if its pink it's good."

Casey started dry heaving in a playful way. "Thank you so much. I literally can't say thank you enough."

She wrapped her arms around his neck and squeezed, kissing his cheek. "I love it all! This is not going to fit in my suitcase but I'll squeeze in what I can."

Mr. Hayes chimed in, "I'll mail it to you first thing in the morning. No problem at all."

She got up and hugged all three of them, "Thank you I really do appreciate spending the holiday here. These gifts, the energy. It's been so nice."

"Of course sweetheart," Mrs. Hayes said with her hand on her heart.

As Mr. Hayes collected the discarded paper, Mrs. Hayes

was watching one of the many televised Christmas parades. She and Denver were taking selfies under the tree, that would probably remain in their private galleries, never publicly posted. He posed, kissing her cheek as she smiled so hard her gums were showing. Then a Facetime call came in from Calvin.

Mama, Coraline and Gemini were crowded around him on the couch. "Hey sis!"

Denver looked surprised and smiled and waved. "Merry Christmas! I'm Denver! Sorry, Brian." He chuckled as he started to scoot off camera.

"Hey Denver!" Gemini screamed.

"So that's the boy so important to her?" Mama said leaning into the camera.

Casey started to stand up. "I'll take this call from the room." She smiled and excused herself.

"How am I the one that called you, but everyone wants to chime in and ask questions?" Calvin asked as she closed the bedroom door.

"Sounds about right. Have you opened your gifts? I hid them at Mom's so she could put them under the tree."

He beamed. "I did get your gift. How did you know I needed more book ends?"

She shrugged. "Cause you're my book loving brother."

The phone was suddenly yanked out of his hand to show Gemini's face. "Girl! Denver looks A LOT cuter in the daytime. No shade bae."

"None taken. He is cute. The question is are yall still single?"

Casey rolled her eyes at her favorite pair. "Yes WE are." She looked out the window to the snow covered backyard hills. "Even though I love it here. It's so quiet. I didn't realize Atlanta was that loud."

Gemini nodded. "That's how it feels at Aunt Lorriane's house. Just trees and vibes."

"Yea but I love his family. They are supper cool."

"Cooler than us?" Coraline said leaning into the screen.

"No not cooler. Just different. They do things a lot different than us. It's so cute. On Christmas Eve they..." She chuckled to herself. "It's just nice to not have to hide in Pantry."

Mom yelled in the background, "I know! I kept finding books and shit behind the rice."

Calvin and Coraline gave her a look. "Well now you made the block hot."

Casey smiled sheepishly, "Sorry. Merry Christmas yall?"

"Yea yea eat, drink and be merry. Thanks for her gifts!" He said.

"Your welcome!" Then they ended the call.

When Casey went back downstairs, Denver was on the couch listening to a Christmas music. "Where are your parents?"

"Getting ready to leave, we'll have the house to ourselves for a couple hours." Denver stood up from the couch with an outstretched hand and sweet smile, "Will you dance with me? I just put this song on."

"*A Christmas Song*" sung by Nat King Cole was playing.

She twitched and moved her lips around as she slowly stepped towards him. "It's hard for me to say no to a dance." She clasped his hand as he gently pulled her into him, rocking her side to side with his head rested on the top of hers. His hand rubbing her back. She looked up at him, a swelling feeling filled her chest when she looked into the emerald sea of Denver's eyes. He smiled down at her and squeezed her back. They didn't say anything as they swayed. Nat's rich voice filled the room around them. Casey exhaled.

This was it.

This was the Christmas joy.

Her head was rested on Denver's chest and his chin rested on her forehead. Then she heard a hum behind her. She lifted her head and turned around, it was his parents watching them and smiling.

She chuckled as she stepped away, but Denver pulled her closer.

"There is no need to be embarrassed dear." His dad said with a chuckle. "Merry Christmas to you both again."

His parents left and they went back into their rooms to cuddle and watch Christmas movies and talk, Casey found herself staring at Denver.

"What?" he asked.

She shrugged, "I'm just really happy." He smiled wide as he looked her in the eye, lifting her chin and giving her a soft kiss. The kiss grew into something deeper, a reminder a hope. Before Casey thought too deep into it, she threw her leg over his lap running her fingers through his hair taking off her shirt.

Merry Christmas baby.

AS CASEY SAT in her seat on the plane, all she could think about was how Denver's chest felt under her cheek. How his smile grew when she walked into the room. How when he looked at her, it made her feel like he would do anything and everything she asked even if it meant he breathed the same air she did. His family welcomed her with a customized robe with her initials so she could match them and feel included.

I'm not his girlfriend.

I'm not his girlfriend.

Then what am I?

CHAPTER 14

GEMINI PLOPPED down on Casey's couch as Calvin looked through her fridge.

"So you had to bring him along huh." She said with a chuckle.

"And me miss out on the tea? You know me better than that. It'll be like I wasn't even here."

Gemini scooted closer to Casey. "Alright so you've been back for like three days with an endless smile on your face. What happened? Describe it to me. I want every single fucking detail."

She looked out her window to the business of the streets. "It was... still. It was quiet, relaxing, his parent's house was gorgeous. We had a breakfast buffet, his mom showed me the stables and horses. The house was on acres. But they were also corny in a cute ass way. Like girl they did an actual CHRISTMAS DANCE ROUTINE."

Gemini's jaw dropped as did Calvin's.

"Aww that's cute!" He said. "Gem?"

She shook her head. "Uh uh don't think so. Like matching sweaters and everything?"

"I'll be right back." Casey came back and showed them the emerald stitched robe. "His mom did the stitching herself. I thought for a hot second of seeing a different last name on there."

Gemini pretended to throw herself off the couch. "Did you just say that out loud? Did you tell him that being that lovey-dovey-cozy made you feel this way?"

She took a moment and really thought about what she said. The Christmas energy was screwing with her wires. "How about I go pop more popcorn?"

Gemini made a face, "Now your trying to deflect. Mmmhm that's okay. I see you." The three of them enjoyed watching romantic comedyies. When it got late, they walked out the door with long hugs and hidden yawns.

CASEY RANG in the new year with Calvin and Gemini. The library hosted a 'Ball Drop' night with fireworks and Casey went to support, but all it did was make her think about Denver. How his face looked on the screen when they Face-Timed, how sexy he looked in the kitchen while cooking, even how he cuddled her at his parent's house. She craved it. *No I don't, who wants to be tied down? Not me.*

When the couples kissed at Midnight, she raised her glass and took a shot of Hennessey. The single life. Denver offered to fly in, for New Years but she refused. Not because she wouldn't have enjoyed it, but because she would've enjoyed it too much. They weren't dating. They weren't exclusive. Her phone pinged as she was about to doom scroll.

> Denver: Happy New Year's to one of my beloved 'friends'! I hope your year was as amazing and beautiful as you.

WELL SHIT.

Now she needed a distraction. She texted Ayden to see if he was in town and he responded quickly with a simple, yea and his address. No Happy New Year, no pleasantries. As she was beginning to leave the library Gemini tapped her shoulder.

"Leaving without saying goodbye?"

Casey faked a smile. "Yea you and my brother are making me sick. Then Greg and his fiancé are making me sicker. We'll hang out though."

Gemini frowned, "Okay let me know when you make it home." She hugged Casey tighter than she hugged back. She wasn't in the mode for love.

CASEY KNOCKED on Ayden's door. He opened it wearing basketball shorts with no shirt. "You got money in your pocket?"

She opened her purse, "I've got a couple of dollars. Why?"

"The first person to walk in the house has to have money in their pocket?"

Casey rolled her eyes, "I thought a *man* had to walk through the door with money in his pocket on New Years."

"Person, man, whatever. I'll do it after you just put the money in your pocket."

She pressed her lips in a thin line, "Aight." She put the

money in her pocket and walked through the door. The feeling of familiarity filled her as she walked into the house. She used to do homework on that same couch in high school. She'd had countless dinners at their dinner table. There were still family photos on the wall, same furniture in the same place for over 10 years. "I love how your moms house hasn't changed a bit."

Ayden nodded looking around, "Yea that's another reason why I hate staying here but oh well." He shrugged. "I usually get a hotel but I'll save some bread since Mom's in the Bahamas."

Casey gasped, "What? Not out the country! Alright Ms. Jones."

"Mmhm, like she's fancy."

She hummed as she smelled the black eyed peas in the crockpot. "Oh so you were cooking huh."

"Yea that's the only way."

"It's too late for me to eat but that's cool."

Ayden chuckled as he walked to his bedroom and she followed. It still had football and basketball posters up like it was 8 years ago. It made her feel nostalgic and sick at the same time. As much as she loved that version of him, that boy was long gone.

She was with a man.

She opened the drawer next to his bed on the nightstand, his loaded gun. "Yea I still keep it in the same spot, just in case." She sighed and closed the drawer. She hated that shit. They cuddled in bed, his arm wrapped around her. Even though it felt familiar, Denver's arms felt safer, calmer.

"It's been cool chillin with you. Reminds me of a simpler time, even though you wouldn't let me get this far. You wouldn't let anybody fuck back then."

She scoffed, "You right. You weren't about to trap me. You

can only do so many moves when your pregnant. My body is right and you aren't about to ruin it."

Ayden nuzzled his nose in her neck. "Mmm that sexy ass body." They laughed together.

BAM!

The front door hit the wall and a rush of heavy footsteps followed. Casey's shoulders tensed up as she turned to look back to Ayden; a hard look crossing his eyes. By the time he sat up on his elbow, he was grabbed out of the bed by five men while Casey screamed and kicked them.

They weren't there for her.

They dragged him by his arms and shoulders to the bedroom floor.

"Stop it!" she screamed.

They ignored her. The men were masked wearing all black, all beating Ayden at the same time. He coughed and curled up in the fetal position as the blows landed on him.

She was shaking. *Fuck! What do I do, what do I do?!* She flinched when she heard a crack from Ayden and his groan.

Suddenly, her father's large mean frame came to her mind and his voice reminded her, "Your Bull's daughter! Show 'em! Aint no punk on your blood!"

Her heart was beating out of her chest. The nightstand.

She reached across the bed and quickly pulled open the drawer. She grabbed the cold metal and pulled it out. His chrome plated 9mm. She made sure it was loaded.

Daddy's lessons.

She cocked the gun back and the men stopped. Just the sound made them freeze. Ayden was still curled up on the floor with his hands around his head, blood leaking from between his fingers.

She pointed the gun at them. "I said get off of him." She said sternly.

"Fuck! Is that Casey Grant?" one of the men mumbled.

"Yes its me, bitch!" She yelled. "I know you motherfuckers know who I am and who my daddy is. I hope I don't have to make a phone call to Fulton County to bother him because someone bothered me. Now I *heavily* suggest yall back away from him."

They slowly backed away with their hands up.

"Don't flinch. I'd hate to leave a mess. Put your backs up against this wall."

They did and made side glances at each other.

"Take off your masks too."

They froze not moving. Casey put the gun up to one of their heads. "If yall don't take off your fucking masks, your moms can see your face in your casket. Take. Them. The. Fuck. Off."

They took off their masks and Casey recognized them instantly. They were regulars at the club and use to 'work' close with her dad.

"James, you should be more careful. I'd hate for your daughter to become an orphan. Your baby mama was killed last year." Her eyes darted back and forth looking at each other with a grimace and no fear. "Same for the rest of you. Ayden is under the protection of the Grants. If anyone has a problem with it, they can see my daddy cause I *will* be calling him. Get the fuck outta here."

They hurriedly left Ayden's room and slammed the door behind them. This is why she didn't want to get involved in this shit.

Even though her mom sent her to the best schools on the 'good' side of town, her blood was tied to this business. The business her father started when he invested into Mama's business with dope money when she bought a second location.

What Casey never told Calvin or Coraline, was that she

tried to have a relationship with her father, even though he had been locked up and wouldn't be out anytime soon.

Being found with thousands of kilos of cocaine and pounds of marijuana with intent to sell and the murder charges are what got him caught up. Then when the cops found a nine year old working for him, that was the nail in the coffin. More blood on his hands. He was one of the biggest king pins in the city, that was still feared. Hell, she was scared of him just his face and the stories around him. Once she was old enough to visit him she did. But only once. She tried to not think back on the conversation.

She quickly walked over to the kitchen and wet a towel with cool water, then went to Ayden, still on the floor, breathing slow. She placed the towel on his swollen and cut cheek. "Do we need to go to the ER?"

He coughed and groaned. "No I'll be a'ight, shit." He tried to roll over. "Just help stand up."

Casey reached for his hand and helped him up. Most of his weight was on her and she walked him to the bed. "Lay down, I'll check the medicine cabinet."

She went into the bathroom and grabbed Band-Aids, alcohol patches, ibuprofen and more cool wash clothes. The room was silent as Casey tore open the pack of ibuprofen and emptied it in his hand. She bandaged the cuts she saw and put ice packs on his bruises. Ayden occasionally hissed, but she could feel his embarrassment.

He got jumped in his childhood bedroom.

She knew she wasn't going to be able to go back to sleep. The mood was gone. So she tucked him into the bed and went into the living room. She turned on the lamp and dimmed it so it wouldn't shine in his room. Then she went to the one app she knew would kill hours of time, Kindle. Forcing herself to read book after book would lessen the tension from her spine. But she still glanced at the door.

That damn door.

She didn't know the night would turn like this. But hearing Ayden's snores brought some comfort. *I almost lost him again.*

CHAPTER 15
AYDEN

WHEN I WOKE UP, Casey was getting dressed. Then the pain and memories hit. The attack, the swelling and throbbing throughout my body. *Fucking bullshit.*

"I didn't mean to wake you. I didn't want to leave with the door unlocked."

I nodded, my ears still ringing from the blows that landed from those assholes. "I'm sorry, Case. You know I never want to bring you into this."

"Yea," she whispered. "I'm still going to call my dad though."

I knew she didn't want to do that, hence why I never mentioned Bull. But I can assume she hasn't visited him in awhile. I got up slow and limped, trying to walk her to the door.

"Let me know when you make it home, aight?" The year just started and I didn't need her pulled into anymore mess.

She nodded, "Yea sure. Have a good day and take it easy."

How was I still paying the price for what happened to me as a kid? I didn't snitch and served my time. I only went a few places while I was in town. Someone must have been watching me, tailing me during my visits. Then to have the balls to do it in front of a Grant, in my own mother's house.

Whatever message they sent had been received, painfully. I wasn't about to bother Casey anymore. She looked like she didn't get any sleep. If it wasn't for the pain, I would've followed her home. So I texted the only other person I could think of.

Ayden: I need some help *sends location*

Greg: The crib? Be there in 15

GREG WALKED in with his gun in his waistband. When he walked into the bedroom and saw what shape I was in, he did a walkthrough of the place to make sure it was empty. Then looked out the window. After I broke down everything that happened, Greg cursed more than a few times.

"The fuck goin on? That's fucked up. What you need me to do?"

"Make my ghosts to stop chasing me. I want my hands to be clean. But a glass of water would be straight right now," I grimaced, trying to laugh through the excruciating pain.

Greg nodded as he walked towards the kitchen and came back with two glasses of water. "The only person who made it out clean was Dre. He said it was for his kids and nobody has heard from him since. I think that nigga is out the country in Columbia or something."

I winced as I sat up in the bed taking the glass Greg. "This is why I left in the first place. I especially didn't want to bring Casey in this shit. She doesn't deserve that. She never did. Her dad is already doing time. She doesn't talk about it, but I know it bothers her."

Greg took a swig of his water. "I get it. Nobody has tried me in awhile. I'm sorry this situation happened man. It was unnecessary as hell, just young hot shit."

"It was. What if they took her bruh? I wouldn't be able to call Coraline or their Mama with that shit. They're the reason everything has died down. How did they even do it?"

Greg leaned forward, "I heard one million showed up on a couple doorsteps with a note advising peace. All groups agreed and created zones for themselves."

"Money talks I guess."

I was still bothered by the situation. I prayed to stay safe in jail. I didn't think it would creep to the outside after all this time. I didn't even give information.

Greg sat with me for the rest of the day. I was finally able to get up from the bed and go to the bathroom by myself so there was no need to go to the ER.

I had to speak to someone from my past that might help, though.

I GROANED SITTING in the seat in front of the glass. I heard the buzz of the doors opening and slamming on the other side. I tried to not flinch.

The door.

Then the 6'5" 300 pound inmate stepped into the room with a smile as he picked up the phone. "Well. That's a face I didn't think I'd see. What brought you back, nigga? From the look of your face you got a warm welcome." Bull laughed, his vibration bouncing off the glass.

I winced crossing my arms, "Wassup Bull. Some shit went down last night. Your daughter was there."

He stopped laughing as a serious look crossed over his face. The bull was released. "Casey?" He whispered into the phone, his teeth starting to grind.

I nodded.

"What happened? Is she okay?" He squeezed the phone tighter as his frown grew.

"She's aight. Held the gun to all of their faces to get them off me. They stormed my mama house. Disrespectful fucks."

Bull began scratching his chin, his tattooed knuckles in view spelling PAIN. "They're supposed to leave my baby girl out of this. Even if she won't visit, she still has my blood." He nodded to himself. "Give Oldie a call and let him know what happened. Today."

I nodded. "Already done, boss."

Bull nodded, then solemnly shook his head. "I knew I should've kept you outta this shit. Casey was looking for your ass at graduation. I shouldn't have brought your young ass in this. You did your time though."

"Yea. Did my bid and went back to school. I'm a pharmacist now."

Bull's chuckle was low and like gravel. "Nigga, your joking. A pharmacist? Shit I should've done that. Gone to school and get my ass beat when I come back to town. Instead of staring at these fucking walls." He chuckled. "I'll take care of it. Give Casey a hug for me. Her old man still thinks about her."

A loud buzzer rang above them. Bull slowly rose from the chair that squeezed as he rose to his full build. He brought the phone closer to his mouth, "Put something on that eye too boy, it's swollen."

I didn't know if I would pass the message to Casey, but I did feel better about the situation being handled.

What else could I do?

CHAPTER 16

CASEY DIDN'T WANT to talk to anyone the entire week. Coraline let her work from home, so she did. She didn't respond to Ayden or Denver's texts. There was too much shit going on in her head. What do you say to the man you watched get his ass beat? She didn't even know if he would survive the night. When he did, she left. *I need to pick up, right fucking now.*

She texted Greg to ask if he wanted to match and she that needed some. He agreed and arrived in her parking garage a few minutes later.

Casey pulled on her hoodie and leggings, grabbed her phone, wallet and blunt. When she walked into the parking garage, she saw Greg's car immediately. The cold January air didn't torture her body long when she made it to his passenger door.

"Tell Casey I said wassup bitch." The women said in the car speaker.

"Hey hoe," she laughed. Amber, Greg's fiancé was cool.

She and Casey had hung out a few times, but they weren't like, best best friends. They had history, but it wasn't disrespectful. Greg and Amber had been poly for a few years now.

"I'll talk to you later girl."

Greg pulled out of the garage and pulled into the near by park. The sun was just beginning to set so the cold Atlanta sky was showing the beautiful portrait of orange and pink. She stared into a cloud and lit her blunt just as Greg broke the silence with putting an ashtray in the cup holder.

"So Ayden reached out."

She nodded. She should've known he'd want to talk about it. "I don't really care honestly. But he needs to go to the hospital or urgent care or something. I hated having to do that. He knows how I always felt about the hot shit. I didn't want to be there. I didn't want to see that shit."

Greg nodded as he lit his blunt.

"I went by there and looked out for him. He's up and moving but his face is still swollen pretty bad. I know that was hard for you. Bull never wanted you to see or sniff that side."

She scoffed as they exchanged blunts. "Yea I sniffed it alright. When my friend wasn't able to graduate because he was in jail. I know you didn't go to those court hearings but I did. When he taught me how to shoot a gun when I was 13 and I was scared! I hated it. He was always scary." She took a deep breath as a tear weld up in her eye. "I sworn on that day that I was going to do everything I could to not have to fire a gun again. I still technically haven't, thanks to a face card. Bull... fucked our family up."

Greg sat silently. He looked out at the sky. "I'm not saying he was perfect. But what I am saying is that he didn't force the guys. Hell Ayden and I wanted to because we were young stupid knuckle heads and convinced Bull to let us in. He took the fall. Forgiveness isn't for the other person, it's for you. Bull just did what he knew, which just happened to be street shit. The street shit also put you in the best schools, the best clothes. He always wanted you to have the best."

Casey shrugged and admired the painted sunset view in front of her. "When was the last time you spoke to him?"

She turned and looked him in the eye to see if he would lie to her. "He calls every couple of weeks or so to check in. He always asks about you."

She scoffed hard, then started to cough. They exchanged blunts again. As the float started to settle in her body, she imagined herself in a blush leotard doing bar combinations on the cloud in pair of fresh chocolate brown pointe shoes, the pain rising from my toes to my calves. She still heard her childhood instructors French accent in her ear as she practiced; *first position, Plié, Relevé *clap* second position, Plié, Relevé *clap** .

Maybe if she just stayed on the cloud, she won't have to think about the look on those boys faces when a gun was pointed straight at their eye.

Her phone vibrated in her lap.

> Denver: Hey I just wanted to check in with you, I know you want your space rn. But whatever it is, I'm here for you 🤍

SHE STARED at her phone and the text.

"You like him huh?" Greg asked driving back to her place, weaving through downtown traffic.

She sighed, "I do. He's nice, will visit whenever I ask. But being long distance has its own hang ups. Then I met his family on Christmas. Fucking Christmas magic and shit. He's been begging me to be official, basically. But I don't know about all that."

He nodded, rubbing his beard as they came up to a red light. "What's stopping you?"

"He literally lives in another state and not on the east coast, a whole different time zone. To do a relationship, let alone long distance. I don't know if it's worth it. There's too much on my mind right now. I don't mean to snap. I just need to get my shit together about this studio, not a boyfriend. Boy toy? Yes, chew and throw."

Greg flinched and chuckled. "Damn chew and throw? I guess. But I eventually got tired of that and 'got my shit together' for Amber. I mean we've been open for a few years, but I wasn't always the best partner. Her happiness and comfort is my main priority. If she wanted to close everything and be monogamous, I would."

"Speaking of, who have you been entertaining lately? We haven't hung out in awhile." Then winked at him.

Greg's face changed into embarrassment as he looked away from her. They drove through another light, right into her parking garage. "Text me when you make it inside."

She nodded and waved as she held her jacket closer to her body. When she opened her door and closed and locked it behind her, she texted Greg that she was inside. He liked the message.

She knew what she had to do.

WHILE CASEY WAS WATCHING a reality show on her couch, Sky texted her to see if she was free to go to the park that afternoon. She welcomed any excuse to leave the house and replied yes before getting dressed.

She saw Sky sitting down near the swings, carefully watching Nettie play with another little girl with beaded braids.

"Hey! Say thank you Nettie!" Sky yelled from the bench. As Casey made her way up the hill.

"Tank you for helping me!" Nettie said with a grin at the other girl.

"You welcome, wanna keep playing?" They nodded and ran back up the slide.

Casey sighed watching them, "I don't know. I might have a kid. They look so cute!"

Sky laughed heartily, "Bitch why would you want to do a stupid ass thing like that? I'm glad I only have one. You think your stressed now? Tuh. She's lucky she made it here. BE CAREFUL!"

Nettie looked at Sky from the top of the jungle gym, putting her hands down the bar.

Casey chuckled with her.

Sky continued as she squinted at Nettie. "Do you like having money? Free time? Hobbies? Your body? Don't let these snot nose kids fool you. I love mine cause she's a blessing but tuh I'll be damned if I start over again. I've already got three jobs. The two that pay me, and her." Sky shook her head. "This shit is hard man, especially alone. But I'll do anything for that little girl." She turns and looks at Nettie lick a pole. "DONT PUT YOUR MOUTH ON THAT!" Sky got up, wipes in hand trying to clean her daughters face.

Nettie gave her mom puppy eyes, a smile, then ran away waving her arms. When Sky returned Casey asked her, "Why of all names did you name her Nettie? Like from The Color Purple?"

Sky laughed. "She's named after my Grandma, Nethel. But everyone called her Nettie for short. She died when I was 20 and I've missed her ever since. Then when I found out I was pregnant a few years later, I knew I had to keep it going. Nethel is her government name, so Nettie it is."

"Such an old name for a baby girl."

Sky laughed and shoved her shoulder.

After two minutes, she ran to Casey. "I I gotta go bathroom."

"Mommy bathroom! Mommy I needa pee! Mommy!"

Sky took a deep breath. "Yes, I heard you baby. Let's go to the bathrooms over there." Casey stood up and grabbed Sky's backpack, tailing them as they ran to the bathroom. Maybe she didn't want kids after all. Rich aunties are necessary right?

When they came back from the bathroom, Nettie played with the other little girl again. But now it was time to go. The other girls dad walked up to pick her up.

"Nettie does need more friends." Sky whispered to herself. "Hey! My daughter loved playing with yours. Y'all live close?"

He shook his head, "Naw naw we don't. This is our first time back in a min. They was shootin on the field. The cops didn't do shit. That's why y'all saw me walking back and forth if you aint notice. 'Lanta fucked up right nah."

They turned to look at each other. "Shootin?! I didn't hear about that. That's crazy" Sky asked, her hand on her hip.

Nettie tugged Sky's shirt. "Mommy! Mommy when are we leaving?"

"In a second baby."

The man continued. "Yea man! I saw y'all sittin over there calm. It happened a couple days ago. But the sun is starting to go down so we about to clear out, too. I'll take ya number so we can meet at the park and what not."

Sky eyed the man up and down, then. "Mmm. I'm sure there are safer parks somewhere." Sky and Casey nodded.

Nettie continued to yank harder on Sky's shirt until she turned her neck and gave her a death stare as she handed the man her phone. Nettie froze. "What's your daughter's name?" Casey asked.

He smiled, "Zaria, I named ha afta my wife."

Sky grinned back as he handed her phone back. "That's a beautiful name! We'll set something up so they can play. Nettie, tell Zaria bye."

"Bye," Nettie whispered as Zaria waved back, walking with her father hand in hand. Nettie got in the stroller and Sky rolled away. Casey helped her load the stroller in the car.

"Well imma head out, get dinner out the crockpot before the babysitter comes to watch Nettie for the night. You alright?"

Casey nodded, knowing she couldn't use Sky as her sounding board right now. How could she complain when Sky had so much going on already? It wasn't right to complain about what she had going on with Sky stressed enough with her jobs and daughter. "Yea. I'm good. I'm glad nothing bad happened."

Sky shook her head as she closed Nettie's car door. "Me either. Now, I gotta find another park. Still working on a studio name?"

She nodded solemnly, completely forgetting about number 1 on her list. What did business owners do after something traumatic happens? She barely wanted to visit the studio right now. "I'll figure it out eventually." Then a conversation with Gemini popped in her mind. "Oh! I almost forgot. Calvin and Gem need a flower girl for their wedding so I suggested Nettie. Is that okay? Your invited to the wedding of course."

Sky squealed, "Aww! Of course! Can you send me Gemini's number to confirm? I want to ask for the wedding colors and where to get her dress so everything matches. Those pictures are going to be so cute. I need to practice some hairstyles so it's perfect." She looked down at her watch, "Shit I can't be late. I'll talk to you later girl." They hugged tightly, Casey rubbing her back. Sky sighed against her.

"Love you." Casey said with a weak smile.

"Love you too. Call me!"

"I will," she screamed as she got in the car. She didn't pull off until Sky left behind her. She called Denver before driving home and he answered on the second ring, sounding surprised.

"Hey what are you up to?"

"Nothing I just left the park with Sky and Nettie."

"Aww did you have fun?" She heard a pan sizzling in the background.

"Yea I did. Nettie is so cute she just gets into a lot of stuff. Do you see yourself having kids?"

Denver coughed. "Uhh not right now. I need a wife first. I don't want kids out of wedlock and even after marriage I want time to enjoy my wife. Kids require a lot of time, attention and money. I want to love on my woman and spoil her before adding to that equation. Why do you ask?"

She shrugged even though he couldn't see it. "I don't know. So many people are parents so it's easy right?"

He scoffed. "Being responsible for a tiny human that can't form sentences. That sounds hard as hell to me."

"What are you doing? Cooking?"

He paused on the line while she heard dishes. "Yea I'm cooking for uh for one."

Her eyebrow lifted. "For one? That sounds really suspicious."

"Does it? It doesn't to me. Well I have to hop off and eat dinner. We're still on for our call later right?"

"Yea. I guess I'll talk to you then." Then the line ended. Why did he become so defensive all of a sudden? Denver was usually the most open and she knew she heard multiple plates being placed.

He's single. You are single.

She almost forgot.

CHAPTER 17

CASEY WAS in long sleeve yellow shirt with black boy shorts, laying across the foot of the bed. "I could give Denver video call and see was he's up to." The line rung once and he answered.

"Thank you for calling Denver's Dick Workshop, where we are open for one. How many I help you?"

She smiled, her butterflies swirling in her stomach. "Oo a dick workshop. What do you sell?"

"It all depends on what you needs miss lady. Either way, were here to provide."

She rolled her eyes but still loved it, "Mmhm how was your day?"

"It was good. I did a virtual conference today so that was interesting. It was more a jeopardy feel but they enjoyed it. What about yours?"

She twisted her lips, "It was fine."

He gave her a look. "It was fine? It doesn't sound fine. Talk to me."

She sighed. "I'm just thinking about my friends. Gemini and Sky are my girls and I love hanging out with them. But what if something bad happened to them? Sky literally has the cutest daughter and Gemini is about to be my sister in law."

"What makes you think something bad with happen to them?"

She looked away from the camera towards her front door. She found herself checking her locks multiple times to get her heart to stop racing. "Nothing. That was random."

Her sleep hadn't been great since everything with Ayden. This FaceTime was different since it was midnight her time. They usually didn't stay up this late talking. But she was excited about what they were about to be listening to in a matter of minutes. She needed to think about something else. Be somewhere else. "Are you ready?" She asked with a fake grin.

"I hope." He gave a nervous smile.

She laughed, "I could've slept over at Gemini and Calvin's. I'm sure they are having their own listening party."

"I can imagine. That's why I'm honored you picked me to listen with."

She rolled her eyes, "I also didn't want to see them suck each others faces off."

Denver smiled, lines showing next to his eyes.

"Okay I'm starting it, you ready? *Cowboy Carter* has officially dropped!" She bounced on her elbows and opened the album.

He pressed keys on his phone, "Now I am."

"I'm so excited, one, two, three now!"

They listened to the entire album together. They smiled, danced, clapped and danced even more. When he grabbed his cowboy hat and started line dancing, Casey laughed the hardest she had in days.

"I'm surprised you actually have rhythm," She jested. "I'm still surprised by your split on Christmas Eve."

Denver made a face in the camera, "I'm still a country boy. We need to go to a bar on Broadway when or if you ever come back to Nashville."

"Let me tell you something, I'm a southern girl but not a country girl. I don't know nothing about that. Keep me in the city. But I loved how quiet it was at your parent's place."

When the album started again, they kept listening in the background. But hearing *Blackbird* again, made her bitterly cry. It surprised both of them. He quietly watched her, trying to comfort her with his eyes. "It's okay to cry, Casey."

She sniffled. "There's just been a lot going on. I really look forward to when we talk because..." She sniffed again. "Because I feel like I can actually relax around you. I was hanging out with Ayden and uh. Things took a turn. It reminded me of the past I've been running away from."

She gave him a look and he encouraged her to keep talking.

"My dad... my dad wasn't a great man. He did some fucked up things that made my family more money, but ruined other families. I visited in him jail when I was 18. I was so dumb to show up in my graduation gown so he could see me. Even when I was going off on him because Ayden was in jail because of him, he smiled. He actually smiled at me and said he was proud of me. I felt so good Denver. Like I finally did something right.

"But why would I fight so hard for his approval? Why did he have a hand in Ayden going to jail so young. He was 18 in jail with grown ass men. He doesn't talk about it but... I hate that my blood came from someone who has caused so much destruction."

A whimpered escaped her mouth, she covered her face with her blanket.

He nodded she knew he wished he was there to hold her. "I think people make mistakes. You don't have to keep them in your life if you don't want to. What I do know, Casey, is that you can conquer anything you put your mind to. You will open your studio. You will be successful. You cannot answer for the sins of your father, that's his story. But you have your own. Your own story that you can control. You can't control the past, but you can control how it shows up in the present. Your family loves you. Your brother and sister love you. I love you."

Casey was stunned. He said it. He actually said it. When her face reappeared under the blanket, Denver realized what he said.

"Thank you." She whispered. "Can we fall sleep together?"

"Of course." They propped their phones on their pillows. "Don't forget to put your phone on the charger. Good night Case."

"Good night Denver."

Then they fell asleep.

That was the best night of sleep Casey had in the new year.

CHAPTER 18

I'M STANDING *in my living room, the gun cold in my hand. The door jiggled, but a man was suddenly behind me with one hand covering my mouth and the other using a knife to stab through my side. I was frozen in pain as four more men stormed my condo. Running right towards me.*

Get down!

Shut up bitch!

Their sneakers beating into my body and hands as my vision blurs.

"FUCK!" Casey said with a scream. Then listened to the emptiness of her home. The buzz of the fan, the dripping of rain on the porch.

I'm fine. I'm fine.

CASEY WAS STANDING at her desk in her office at the Grant Enterprises corporate building. It was lifted so her keyboard was in the perfect position. She was mindlessly playing with her feet practicing going from 1st position to 5th position on each foot 10 times. She was supposed to be on a system-wide call, but she was reviewing business logos.

She had finally thought of a name, the Passion Pole Studio. This studio is her passion brought to life and she hoped other people grew a passion for dance as well. She submitted the business application and started the copyright processes. Even though she wasn't sleeping and sometimes couldn't stop her hands from shaking. She was going to accomplish her dream.

She decided that she needed a team of five instructors and a front desk attendant in order to get started. How would she pay them? She had no clue. Maybe they could volunteer and use the space to record their content until she had enough revenue to put them on official payroll? Or maybe apply for grants or business loans to get temporary contractors?

She heard something drop behind her. Her heart dropped. *Watch the door, keep your eyes open.* She turned around, and it was just a binder that tipped over on her bookshelf. A breath escaped her chest as she slowed her breathing to calm down.

She'd had the same nightmare over and over for three months now. The only night it didn't come was when she fell asleep with Denver on FaceTime. No matter what she did or how fast she tried to run, she still gets jumped and screamed awake. She and sleep hadn't been spending much time together. She was too scared to look up PTSD and it's symptoms. *What if I' a textbook case?* She wasn't going to force Denver to be on the phone with her every night when he was in a different time zone, she didn't want him to even know about her family drama. That was way too personal. She hoped the bags under her eyes were hidden away from the layers of makeup.

Coraline slammed the door to Casey's office. She jumped, abruptly being brought back to reality. Her heart instantly began to race as her knee shook.

The door. The door.

When Casey noticed Coraline frown, it stopped her stomach from spinning. "So you didn't want to join the company call? We went over some important stuff and the manager at the L.A. club wants you to give her a call."

"Well damn. First off, good afternoon. Second, I was viewing logos for the studio. I finally got a name! Now there's so much to do now that hump is over. I didn't even realize what time it was."

Coraline's face got even more serious. "Calvin was even on the call. What's going on with you?"

She pushed her chair out, "You know I'm opening this studio in like a month. All I have is a space, no consistent teachers except Sky and me. Then I have to order some tint for the windows so that creeps don't try to watch the classes and get a free show. I'm thinking about shit that you don't even care about. Shit I'm gonna to have to pay for."

Her sister's shoulders rose then fell, "Look. If anyone knows how hard it is to run a business. It's me. So I get it. But also, too bad so sad. Sometimes you have to juggle 30 different things and not break a sweat. You're a Grant, you'll be aight."

She gave her a deadpan stare. "Thanks for the great advice, sis."

Coraline brushed the shoulders of her blazer, "That's what I'm here for. But don't miss another meeting. I'd hate to look for a replacement."

She cut her eyes to her older sister. "Whatever."

"Come by my office before the end of the day. When you have the time." She turned on her heel and left.

"WHY DO I have to go right now?! You know my launch is coming up, Coraline. It's literally a couple of weeks away."

In her sharp suit, Coraline shrugged as she sat behind her desk, Mom's old desk. "You still work here. We're going to be launching another New York location by the end of August. I've been interviewing managers for this new club location and just sent an offer. Once our recruiter from Helping Human Helpers sends me the approval, you're going to go out there to train the performers. You know, do your job."

She shook her head no. "This fucks up my whole plan for the next couple of months. How can I run a new pole studio from New York? How long will I be there for training?"

"I thought you liked traveling? Didn't you complain about not being in first class? We had a good fiscal year and holiday season. The Christmas Cookie peep shows were more successful than we thought. I'll make sure you fly *real* comfortable. You'll be there for two months."

Heat started to radiate from her body. If they weren't in that professional setting, she would pull her hair or put gum in it. Some big sister. "What about Calvin and Gemini's wedding!? Or did you forget? Heartless bitch."

She rolled her eyes with a frown. "We are in March, you would be back in May and the wedding is in June. That gives you plenty of time to get situated before the wedding."

Casey crossed her arms and leaned back in the chair. *She did this on fucking purpose.*

Coraline stood up and approached Casey, leaning on her

desk in front of her with her ankles crossed. "What's going on? Your usually asking for the first flight out."

She pressed her lips together, looking away. Her sister was horrible at teetering the mom vs boss vs sister line. Why would she care that she's not able to think about the business she wants? Why would she care that the planning process has been fucking overwhelming? Why would she care about her night-mares? *Her nightmares of being taken, bound and beaten.* Cora-line had always known what to do. That's how it was growing up.

"Nothing, everything is fine. Just send my flight informa-tion I guess. Is there anything else *boss*?" she said with a sigh.

"No, that was it. I'll send your flight information in a couple days."

Casey quickly stood up and stormed out of the office. No goodbyes. No hugs. This fucked up Casey's ENTIRE plan.

Her dream.

She just submitted all that paperwork. The first set of routines have been recorded. She even made the studio more homey by adding a rug and some comfy chairs. She wanted to bring good energy every time she visited the space.

Yet, there was still more that needed to be done. Was it this hard for Mama? When she told her success story, she made it sound like it was three easy steps, not 50.

Fuck. She raced home, dodging around cars and speeding past yellow lights. She slammed the car door and pouted the whole way to her front door. As soon as she saw her couch, a wail escaped her throat. She had to let out the frustration of having to change *everything* because her sister said so.

No pole work today.

She covered herself with a blanket, from her head to her feet. She didn't even want a glass of wine right now. Maybe this dream just wasn't meant to come true. Maybe her nightmares were coming to life.

CHAPTER 19

A STRING VERSION of *"Not like Us"* played on the speakers throughout the restaurant. The bar crowd was dressed in an array of linen shirts and large skirted dresses, completely in character. A woman even dyed her cornrows pink to match her long flowy corset dress. Her baby hairs, too. As she was sitting down at the table, he approached before he turned on his mic. "Hey, your hair is amazing."

She winked, "Thank you."

Brian winked back. The crowd charm was on. "I'm your host for *Bridgerton* Trivia night! Art thou readth to answer some questions? The grand prize is a $50 dollar gift card for each team member! If it will please the court, it is time for the first question. Who wrote the book series that the show is based on?"

The teams huddled together and whispered as they wrote on a white board.

"Alright put em up!" The groups held up the boards while also reviewing the others. "Table 1 and 3 are correct which means we have a tie! The answer was Julia Quinn." Both tables erupted into cheers as they high fived each other. But they were not heard since they were wearing gloves.

"That was the last question of the night. Both table winners, please see the manager at the bar for your gift cards." The group of women skipped quickly, eager with excitement.

In an exaggerated British accent he said. "My dearest participants, you have a an exquisite crowd."

Everyone applauded as the groups stood up, some left right after while others lingered.

Either way, his gig was officially over. He was standing at the bar when he felt a tap on his shoulder.

"You did a great job tonight, can I buy you a drink?" The blonde hair woman said with a wink.

"Sure," he said with a weak smile. He couldn't turn down a free drink. He still needed to collect the rest of the money. "You're here with the event right?"

She looked down at her chest and dress then back at him. "Is it this dress that says 'my husband died in his sleep and I'm in the hallway with a candle'?"

He chuckled as he sat down with a stool in between them. "I mean my neck itches from this shirt," he shrugged. The bartender took his drink order and began making his whisky shot.

"So have you been doing this long? This is my first time coming here."

He shrugged. "A couple years. I like making people laugh."

"Well I like laughing. Can I bring you home to my husband? We would have so much fun with you." She brushed her hand across his chest. "I can pay you."

He moved her hand off of him. One of those. Must be another Country Cheeks fan but he wouldn't say it out loud. "No I'm okay."

"Oh come on!" she yelled drunkenly. "Be the caramel to our vanilla Sunday?"

He got up from the stool and put cash on the bar. He didn't want to owe anything to her. "Uhh I'm gonna go." He quickly moved from the bar to the restaurant manager.

"Brian! Great job man. You always rock the house. I can't believe this many people dressed up." He handed him the envelope.

He smiled widely as he reviewed the check and tucked it into his pocket. "Yea, me either. I'm glad it wasn't just me. See you in two weeks."

"See you then B!"

As he was about to walk out, he noticed pink cornrows making eye contact and smiled. Was that an invitation to walk over there? He smiled back and gave her a head nod. She waved him over and made room for him. Bet.

He walked over to the table and said with the accent, "Good evening, my good lady. Is this seat taken?"

The woman wiped out a fan, from somewhere, and started fanning herself. "My good sir, why of course not."

He smiled wider as he sat down.

"Beautiful evening to be sitting next to a beautiful lady. But alas, what do you call yourself?"

She extended her hand in a cup position so her knuckles were facing him. "Taylor, my lord. And you?"

He kissed her hand twice and met her eyes. "Lord Brian my lady." They laughed loudly together, her tan cheeks blushed.

She stopped her accent. "Well Brian it's nice to meet you. You did great keeping the energy up tonight. I bet you have a woman at home that enjoys all that laughter."

He frowned, then tried to fix it. "I actually don't. I'm as single as a dropped pringle unfortunately. What about you?"

She shrugged. "Men usually pretend to be gentleman,

when they are not. Would you call yourself a 'proper gentleman'?"

He squeezed her hand and he let it go. "I would call myself that. I just spend my days working and writing jokes." He couldn't talk about his OnlyFans account, not after he was just found out.

"Writing jokes?" She asked.

"Yea I'm contracted with Helping Human Helpers so I travel across the country for their employee engagement seminars. But I will say I do my best work in the late hour so I stay up late most nights." He winked at her.

She eyed from again and licked her bottom lip. "Most nights, hmm? What are you doing tonight?"

He grazed his teeth on his bottom lip against the back of his lip. "Nothing after this. What about you?"

She shook her head, adjusting her seated position in the booth. "Nothing."

A server approached their table, "Hello! Is there anything else you would like tonight?"

Taylor looked at her with a smile and slyly glanced at Brian, "Not that I can get here, no. May I get the check?"

The server smiled, "Of course! I'll send the receipt to the tablet on the table so you can pay." Once she walked away, they began eying each other again.

He asked Taylor, "So where are you from?"

"I'm from everywhere. My mom and dad were both in the Army so I was born in Germany and basically moved around with them." She shrugged. "I learned to have fun with each new place and to make a friend or two. What about you?"

"Nashville," He said in a country twang.

Taylor fanned herself again and leaned back in the chair. "Oh a country boy! You might be a real gentleman after all. Tell me about your parents."

Brian laughed louder as he tipped an imaginary hat. "I know how to treat a lady. I watched my dad do it for almost 30 years. They just celebrated their 30 year wedding anniversary and they still act like they got married yesterday."

Taylor smiled, "Aww congrats! Please elaborate on the lovey-doveyness."

He thought before answering as he flashed back to his childhood. "The hand holding."

She pulled the table tablet to herself as she began to pay. "Hand holding?"

He nodded. "Yea they hold hands all the time. When they are in the same room as each other, when they argue. It was nauseating. But the older I get, I understand that feeling and crave for it. I mean, the arguments were rare, but even when they happened they still held hands. I would be so confused. I used to think that my mom would be squeezing the life out of his hand when they were made because his hand would turn red. But when I asked him, he said he was squeezing her hand to keep her calm, not to cause her pain. I've never seen my dad hurt my mom, like ever.

"Make a mistake, yes. But never anything intentional. Their honestly model parents, even when I was a dick-headed teenager. Wow, I'm still talking. I'm sorry for that rant."

She smiled at him. "No, please don't apologize. I think how our parents treat us is really important. When it comes to mine, it's hit and miss. When your parents are soldiers, they either want you to be a perfect solider too or not have time to check on you. But I think the fondest memory I have with them are the road trips. My mom and dad would swap the wheel every 4 hours. Then, when I became 16, I joined the rotation. Even when my younger sister turned 16, she was promoted too." She chuckled to herself. "It was the worst because of boredom so my dad would think of games. The WORSE part of the drive was Texas. That state is huge. I think the only states I haven't visited are on the upper west coast like Washington state. It's on my bucket list to make that trip one day. Now I'm rambling."

His eyes softened. "No I like listening to you talk."

Taylor slid the table tablet back in the corner. "I like listening to you too. Want to finish this convo back at my place?"

"Sure, let me get your number." They exchanged numbers and she send him her address.

"See you soon," she said rising out the seat with a wink. He watched her walk away, her waist complemented by the pink cornrows. He was single, but why did Casey cross his mind still.

He went back to Taylor's place for a cup of coffee that turned into some kissing, nipple sucking and fucking *with protection of course.* He tried to fuck Casey out of his mind but was unsuccessful. Eventually, he became more focused on pounding into Taylor's spine. Trying to get the sound of Casey's moaned out of his head.

No whispers, no making out during strokes. Just sex.

The next morning, Taylor greeted him with a kiss and offered to cook him breakfast. He declined and returned to his home. Glad that he was close to his house, rather than another hotel room.

Home.

He was single, even though his heart didn't feel like it.

CHAPTER 20

THE SUN WAS BURNING through her window as she squinted awake. She looked at her watch. 7:00. It was still morning and she felt like hours had passed from the crying nap. She went to her bathroom and looked in the mirror. Her eyes were puffy, her nose was red.

She did not look her best.

She finally looked at her phone. Missed texts and FaceTimes.

Ayden: Aye my flight is at 10 this morning. Can I treat you to some good food, Casey Cake?

Denver: *Missed Facetime*

Denver: Hey! Call me when you get the chance. I just wanted to check in with you

Mama: Hey sweetie! Call me when you can.

. . .

MAMA WAS DEFIANTLY TRYING to do damage control and she didn't want to hear it. She called Denver back. She looked too horrible to FaceTime and wasn't ready for him to see her 'I've been crying all night because I'm crashing out' face.

"Case! How are you?" He sounded like he had been up awhile.

"Isn't it crazy earlier in Colorado right now?"

"Yea, but I'm just coming back from the gym. How are you? Something sounds different in your voice."

She sniffled, "Fine I guess. Even though Coraline is fucking my life over, again."

"What happened?" he asked concerned. She told him everything that happened and her having to go to New York in a few weeks. "Aww baby that's upsetting. You want me to fly out and make you feel better?"

"Please?" She said with a sniffle. She needed to be in his arms. She needed his comfort. On top of everything and now this?

After giving Denver more details about the forced work trip Coraline orchestrated, they hung up, and she began stress-cleaning her condo. She scrubbed the sink with a toothbrush, dusted the ceiling fans and mopped the walls. After finishing the bathroom, she forgot Ayden texted and invited her out. He was in town and leaving today wanting to treat her to lunch. She replied back asking if four was a good time to meet. When he agreed, she put on a long sleeve crop set with a visor, grabbed her purse and walked out the door. Her Uber was already ordered.

As Ayden and her ate lunch, Denver texted and said his flight landed. She sent her current location and waited for him. She didn't think it was a big deal that he was picking her up, it saved her time and money. After the food and plates were picked up, she noticed Denver walking up to their table.

She smiled widely excited to see him. She didn't realize how much she missed him until they made eye contact. She hadn't seen him in person since Christmas and he still looked great. Her heart started beating fast as a smile grew on her face.

Then his eyes met Ayden's. He immediately looked pissed off. *It's no big deal right?*

Ayden stood up and Denver approached the table, his face burning red. *That wasn't good.* She watched him breathe out his nose when he made it to the table. "Oh this is your lil boy I met at your birthday." Casey raised her eyebrows as she leaned her head and looked at Ayden.

Denver rubbed his hands together. "I ain't a boy," sizing him up. "And nothing about me is little, nigga."

"Nigga? Bruh you're barely black. Shut up witcho light skinned ass. Quincy-lookin ass nigga. Bright ass boy, fuck you talkin' bout."

Denver's nose scrunched up. "Barely? Didn't you start the new year with an ass whooping? Cause I'm about to give you a spring special. Quit playin wit me."

Casey walked around the table and put her hand on Denver's chest. "Can y'all chill?" Looking between them. "It's not that deep and this isn't a competition."

Ayden scoffed. "I never said it was." His arm rested around the back of Casey's chair.

Denver rolled his eyes, "I'm too grown to go back and forth with a 'former' felon." He fixed his shirt. "Casey, let me know when you're ready. When *you* sent me your location, you said you were." Then he turned on his heel and walked away. Her hand limply falling beside her.

Casey gave Ayden a sympathetic look. "Go ahead to your

man," he said. "I got the bill. I'll see you later." She quietly nodded as she grabbed her purse from the table, then gave him a quick side hug. Ayden squeezed her back. "Take care," he said in her ear.

She gave him a weak smile, "Take care and fly safe." She caught up to Denver and tried to slide her hand in his, he gave her a pained look when he snatched his hand away. When they made it to the rental car, he still opened the door for her and helped her in. Even though the hurt was still written in his face.

He got in the driver's seat and started the car. "Why am I here, Casey? You made it seem like you were having a rough time and I caught the next flight out to see you. I was the last person at my gate. I *barely* made it. Then I turn the corner and you're with *that* guy again? What the hell? Once again I looked stupid as fuck. Are you dating him? What is going on? I didn't waste my money for this."

Her bottom lip quivered, "I'm happy to see you Denver. If you believe it or not, I did miss you. That's why I wanted to see you. I haven't seen you in person in three months, since Christmas." She rubbed her hand up his arm. "This long distance is messing with me, okay? I didn't even know Ayden was in town. The rest of the time will be quality time, with just the two of us. I told you our families are close. He worked with my dad... it's complicated but it's not that. I promise it'll only be the two of us till you leave. Okay?"

He scoffed as he pulled out of the parking garage. "Quality time. Since you checked on your other man, huh."

"Bruh drop it." Casey said annoyed.

"Did he fly in to see you too? Do you let him fuck you raw, too?" His hand wiped the bottom of his nose. "You know what, I don't even want to know. You're single right? I'm just who you call when you need a little pick me up, but no commitment. Since I'm single too, right?"

"Yo! I said drop it Denver! Shit! I asked you if this was something you could handle and you said yes. But you just showed your ass to my friend." Casey stared out of the window.

"I know you don't have an attitude after what I just walked into. I didn't even get a heads up. I just walked into the shit and see you laughing and giggling. You could've told me."

She didn't respond. Her chin digging into her palm as she tried to focus on the passing buildings and not the pain in the chest.

The hurt.

They were silent the rest of the ride to her condo. He snatched the bag from the back seat as he walked behind her, still quiet. Casey opened the door and held it open for him, still unable to look him in the eye.

He went into her bathroom and locked the door. She heard the shower get started, while rock music played. She hated seeing him upset. The uneasiness in her gut didn't feel right. Maybe she shouldn't have asked him to come. He has his own job, his own place. And he dropped everything to come to her. She never did that for him.

Ever.

Even though she was single, Denver had gone out of his way multiple times for her. Now, it was her turn to show him that she did care about him.

She pulled down a cookbook from her built in bookshelf. She had to cook something so good that it took him off his feet. This was her first time ever cooking for someone else, a man. She pulled some chicken thighs, butter, carrots, celery and an onion from the fridge, then grabbed some potatoes out of the pantry. This was a dinner that had to impress.

~

SHE OPENED THE PATIO DOOR. His face was rested in solid lines. "Hey, um, I cooked dinner for us. I hope you're hungry."

He nodded and came inside. He sat at the counter in the kitchen. Casey placed the plate of pan-seared chicken with garlic mashed potatoes and sautéed veggies. He took a bite and his entire body softened. "Damn this is good. The chicken is really succulent. I think this is the first time I've had your cooking."

"This is the first time any guy has had my cooking, outside of family."

He looked up at her and nodded. "No need to do something special for me. Haven't you heard *I'm just a friend.*" He sang at the end.

She threw a balled up napkin at his head. "You're gonna keep rubbing it in, huh?"

He stood up, "*Baby you got what I need. But you say I'm just a friend.*" He began waving his hands in the hair, "But you say I'm just a friend. Come on!"

Casey hollered, "Not the song! Your so annoying."

He sat back down." I couldn't hold it in that time. Seriously I do appreciate it. You are special to me and I like spending time with you. I'm sorry about what happened today, your sister assigning you to go to New York right before your business launch. You'll figure it out! Sky is still here; she can help and check in on the place. You have people in your corner, baby."

"Yea, I guess. Calvin has helped me so much, I don't know if I can thank him enough. Sky has been really helpful. I wouldn't have even known about the business paperwork thing.

How did I miss that? But you're right. " She took a bite of the food and moaned, "Oh I did that."

He smiled at her as he put another fork full in his mouth. "Yes, you did. How do you expect me to not be sprung when you can cook like this? Now I'm really going to crash out."

She shrugged and continued eating. She wasn't ready to give the real reason why yet.

The next morning they went to the gym together. It was on the 12th floor of the building. Casey wanted sometime out of her place.

"What are you gonna work on?" Denver asked putting his bag in a locker.

Casey shrugged retying her shoes. "Cardio, I'm gonna head to the treadmill."

Since the gym was two levels. Denver sat above her at a distance on a bike. Pretending to look out the window while Casey began to jog, her ponytail bouncing along with her ass. He couldn't help but find her in a mirror or around the corner. Every move she did was smooth and controlled. When she watched her form and corrected herself on the stair master was impressive.

Denver noticed her eyes on him too while he lifted a dumb bell over his head.

While at their lockers, her clutch fell at her feet. Denver bent down and picked it up on one knee and hands it back to her. "Here's your... bag." He said with a chuckle. When he looked down at his stance he slowly got up and smiled at her.

The rush. She felt the rush of being proposed to. Ohhh my gosh. Then she realized she was staring at him.

"Sorry sorry," she grabbed the pink Coach clutch. "Thanks. Ready to head back?"

"Yea right behind you beautiful."

She turned around and smirked. If only it were like this all the time. Casey absentmindedly grabbed his hand as they walked out the gym, interlocking their fingers together. Denver turned at her surprised and squeezed her hand.

When they made it back to her place, they were pulling each others clothes off. Then when they made it to the bathroom he lifted her on the sink and kissed her. Melting into her tongue like a mint. His hand cradling the back of her neck with her legs wrapped around his waist. They were kissing for so long they didn't even realize the shower wasn't turned on. Their lips were tingling from the friction.

They turned on the water but never left each others touch, scrubbing and kissing the soap away. They dried off and continued kissing in the bedsheets, biting and grabbing any skin they could get their hands on. Back, shoulder, chest, cheek. Then she lifted her head back and looked at him. "I want to try something new, do you trust me?"

He gave her an inquisitive look. "I do, technically." He arched his eyebrow as she reached and opened a box on the dresser. She took out a pair of fluffy pink handcuffs and a blindfold. "Oh this is new. I like it. Who are they for?"

"You," She said licking her lips.

He put his wrist in front of him. "Yes Mrs. Officer."

"Not like that, just some restraint. I'm not gonna role play as a cop."

He laughed as she fastened them on him and placed the key back on the dresser. "Now put your hands above your head."

He raised them up. "I'm ready."

She straddled his hips, swinging the blindfold with a smile.

"Oh were going there. I really like that."

She blindfolded him and made sure his handcuffs were locked. "You okay?"

He hummed, lifting his pelvis so hard his dick brushed against her expecting spot. "Yes ma'am."

"You know you have been very bad, Denver." She brushed her hand across his chest, lightly scratching his abs. "Now you have to be punished. I'll enjoy this but I'm going to make you ache."

He groaned. "Please." His muscles gleaming from the shower water and light filling the room. Casey sat back so his dick sat in front of her. She began massaging it, gently brushing her thumb on his tip. He lifted his hips, aching for the slickness of her mouth. He groaned again. Her other hand stroked him faster and faster as his chest rose and fell against her.

His back began to arch as she slowed her pace, the cuffs rattling. Then she dipped her head down, filling her mouth of him. He growled above her, shaking the handcuffs.

He was gonna go crazy when she set him free. His dick twitched in her mouth and she knew he was close. She pulled away with a loud slurp. "Fuck," he groaned. "I need you Casey."

"Hmm. Fine, since you've been obedient." Casey breathed. She grabbed the key from the nightstand and unlocked him. He removed his blindfold and paused, drinking in all of her features. Her wet juicy lips, button nose and almond eyes. The way her hips curved perfectly to her back. Her cute inner belly button.

He brought his hands to her hips, rubbing circles from her hip, past her core. Then he licked her breast. "I missed you so much," He whimpered.

"I missed you too," she whispered back in his ear. She brought her legs to the side of his hips and lowered herself. A growl escaped Denver's throat as he pulled her even closer, deeper.

She gasped when their pelvises met. He brought his hands

to her head and cradled her face, pulling her in for a passionate kiss. One of those kisses that make you change positions. One of those kisses that make you feel like a puddle under him. When his tongue brushed against hers, while stroking her, she was about to explode. She looked at him above her, intent burning in his eyes. When he punished her nipples, the bomb exploded.

With a loud groan and moan, her nails dug deeper and deeper into Denver's back. Her claws embedded in him as he matched her leaving them covered in her. *Splash.* "Fuck." She said out of breath.

"Fuck," he said looking up at her in awe. "You are so beautiful when you finish. I wish the lock screen on my phone could be the face your making right now."

"With my hair looking like this? I'd murder you. Pictures like these should be locked away, not on your lock screen."

He effortlessly moved her again so her head was slightly off the bed.

"Any face you make, every expression you make should be on display on a museum from how breathtaking you are." She smiled as she lifted and kissed him lightly, a promise.

When her finger brushed his sweet spot behind his ear, it didn't take him long to climax. Then he used every tool she had, her vibrator, rose, cock ring. He gave it to her like he had been holding it in. When he finally went to sleep she couldn't move and dozed off next to him. Her body humming in satisfaction.

When she used the bathroom at 4am, she glances at the new email in her phone. It was the plane tickets to New York. *Might es well see where I'm sitting.* She opened the email and attachment, it was first class. "Well that's the least she could do," Casey whispered to herself.

. . .

AFTER DENVER FLEW BACK HOME the next morning, she already missed him. Later that night while washing dishes, she decided to FaceTime him to see what his fine ass was up to. When he answered he looked like he was caught off guard and getting dressed in his kitchen.

"Why do you look like you just got caught?"

"Bye see you later," a woman's voice said in the background and the door closing.

Casey's jaw dropped. "Oh, so you had a bitch over?"

"Really? After everything? You have no right to be mad right now. Your tagline has been 'we are single.'"

"Well who is she?"

He sighed. "Her name is Taylor, we met at the trivia night event."

She scoffed. "Oh so this has like been a thing. Wow, this is shitty."

"Are you fucking kidding me? You left me, on your birthday, our birthday, to fuck someone else. Now I'm with somebody and you don't like it. Break that down for me, Case. Huh? I thought we were single. Or me picking you up from your 'date' when my flight JUST landed."

She was silent. The pot and sponge fell into the dishwater. She was ironically washing the pot he bought her. "We should take a break from ... being friends. I'll be in New York. I just need to focus right now and you're a distraction."

Denver scoffed. "Wow, your seriously mad. You know what. Fine. You know my number." Then he ended the call.

Her jaw dropped even farther for the fact he hung up on her. "Oh hell no," she said to herself as she dried her hands. She opened the voice recorder and pressed record.

You know what Denv-Brian! I don't give a fuck about us, okay? It was never that serious. I don't care what you do, how you do it, or who you do it with. Fuck you. Fuck ya mama ya daddy fuck you. You piece of shit dick. Yes I'm fucking mad I had to hear it in the background rather than you fucking spelling it out XYZ to me. Fuck you if you didn't catch that earlier. EAT DICK BRIAN!

CHAPTER 21

CASEY WAS STILL MOPING ABOUT GOING to New York. If it was last year, she would've left already. Now she was sad that she didn't know where her business was going and Den-Brian wasn't a thing anymore. She put a variety of outfits in her suitcase. Then she looked at her phone.

INCOMING FACETIME FROM SKY

She answered dryly. "Hello."

"Oh don't worry, I forgive you for not telling me about you leaving for New York NEXT WEEK for two months. Why didn't you text me?" She was walking around her kitchen in a tank top and bonnet.

Casey shrugged. "I didn't want to bother you about it. You have a lot going on."

Sky sighed as she propped the phone on her counter. "Girl, you know you can still talk to me. Right?"

"Yea I know. I just... couldn't find the best time to bring it up. I was supposed to launch the stupid studio this month and now I'm behind behind. I just feel like a failure and a waste.

My mom helped for what? I thought I finally found something for me."

She gave her a sympathetic look. "The love of a mother knows no bounds. Ms. Grant just wanted you to try something and stick to it. That's why she paid it for one year and not 10. It doesn't have to be perfect to get it started. You don't need 17 different classes at launch either. You can grow into it. There is no such thing as an overnight success, sis. This is one of those things where you just have to keep pushing. Even if you don't know where you're going."

Her eyes started to water. "Wow, that was.. really insightful, Sky. I needed to hear that."

"I'm here to support you, too. I can't fuck your brains out like Denver but I'm still here for you." She said with a chuckle.

Casey's heart warmed. She forgot that she had a support system. Not only in her family, but genuine friends too. Calvin came to help her clean up. Sky's advice and encouragement came right when she needed it. While Sky was talking about her day, she checked her phone to see if Denver or Ayden texted her, *neither did.*

NOW IT WAS Sunday and she was sitting across from her selfish inconsiderate sister, eating a Caesar salad with smothered pork chops, rice and gravy. She kept giving Coraline the death stare and her sister wasn't a bit bothered. Calvin and Gemini were having their own conversation and Mama looked between her two girls.

Coraline shrugged as she patted her lips with a napkin. "She's mad a business decision was made. It's done now and she hasn't 'let it go'".

Casey rolled her eyes. "You and I both know it was more

than that. She's is sending me to New York and delaying my business launch!"

The table went quiet. "Honey it's okay! You can still do some work remotely. The world is more technological now."

"Wow Mom you're on her side?"

Calvin gently put his hand on Casey's wrist. "Hey it's okay. I'll check on the studio and everything while your gone."

"That's not fair to you, Calvin. You're literally planning a wedding that's happening WEEKS after I come back. I won't even be able to go dress shopping with Gemini. I have things to take care of, too." Her bottom lip began to quiver but she held it down with her top lip. "It's not fair."

As Mama stood up to walk towards Casey, she was already standing and stepping away from the table. "See y'all at the wedding."

She saw the hurt in her mothers eyes and the shook in everyone else's. It didn't matter. Business was first. She was so mad that she had to release the pressure in her chest because staring at her bedroom ceiling fan wasn't going to do it.

Welp, time to go to the gym. She started on the stair stepper until her knees shook, then threw the weighted balls to the ground for her core. As her body shook, her limit reached, and a growing headache filled her skull. She felt something wet on her lip. When she wiped it, blood was on her sleeve. She tapped her finger at the bottom of her nostril and looked, more blood droplets.

Time to go home.

She quickly took the elevator back to her floor and condo where she could cry as much and as long as she wanted. Her flight was leaving the next morning anyway.

~

FROM HER UBER to the airport, her finger hovered over the call button. She showed her ass in that voice note but she had so much more to apologize for. She listened to alternative music the whole flight to try to get an imaginary think signal to Den-Brian. But even though she was mad, she found herself listening to the songs he played on their first flight together to Atlanta.

She made it to her hotel room at noon. It was a large corner suite with a bar, sitting area with a sectional and flat screen TV and large bathroom with a standing shower. But the only thing Casey could think about was how her dreams were put on hold for the business.

She hated it.

She threw down her bags and kicked them as a furious tear dropped from her eye. Fuck it. She snatched out the bottle of Tequila, and the bottle opener from the counter display.

The first couple of gulps were sour and made her empty stomach burn. But it didn't matter. She brought her phone and the bottle to the couch. Just then, an email came through.

To: Coraline.Grant@GE.com

Subject: NY Training Update

Hello Casey,

I hope you had a good flight! Here is the training schedule you made again, just in case. It's Monday through Friday from 8am to 1pm. But you'll do whatever you want, as you always do. Just get them ready for the opening in 2 months.

Best,
CG
CEO of Grant Enterprises

SHE TOOK another gulp and coughed after. Then put her phone on Do Not Disturb. The last person she wanted to hear from was big CEO sis.

Her jaw started to tingle as a throb started behind her left eye. A silent and desperate cry left her throat as she buried her face under her arms. She had 36 hours before having to appear like her shit was together in front of 30 performers with likely no experience.

She laid her head down on the couch cushion. Whatever.

By the time she sat up and stretched, it was no longer daytime. The throbbing behind her eye wasn't getting any better either.

"Oh Fuck." She looked at her phone.

15 MISSED CALLS FROM MOM
7 TEXTS FROM MOM
1 TEXT FROM GEMINI
2 TEXTS FROM CALVIN
2 TEXTS FROM CORALINE
1 TEXT FROM AYDEN

NOTHING FROM DENVER? She sighed as she opened Gemini's text

Gemini: I know you're still mad. But PLEASE don't worry about missing anything. I'm going to Facetime you when I get the dress fitted so you can see it. And were NOT having the Bachelorette party until you're back. I love you sis

CASEY SMILED at the message and responded with hearts. After she called her mom back, she ignored the rest. She didn't feel like talking that much.

CHAPTER 22

THE FIRST PRACTICE was always the most awkward.

There was nothing like being in a room full of women and the thick aroma of unnecessary competition. Casey had groceries delivered to her hotel room the day before so she could make a breakfast sandwich, an egg and avocado bagel. She wrapped it in aluminum foil and headed out the door. She was wearing a black long sleeve leotard with matching black leggings and Timberlands. In her pink backpack, she had a change of clothes and shoes, cash, and other essentials. The hotel was only three blocks away from the club; it was just surviving the walk there as the icy air cut her cheeks. She threw two bottles of water in her bag, put the hotel key in her wallet and headed out the door.

She gave the hotel attendant a head nod as she walked out into the windy street. Atlanta was usually a little warmer by now. Temperatures under 30 after Christmas was complete misery. The bodies walking through Times Square strode past like she was invincible. She had been to New York enough times to not take it as personal when someone bumps into her and doesn't apologize. There was no southern charm in this cold, hell driven city Coraline sent her to AGAIN. The only good thing about NYC was the fact that she rarely had to drive, which was already never. She either walked or Ubered everywhere.

Walking into the studio, there was a bright neon sign that said 'Opening Soon.' If only *her* studio had that sign on it. If only.

The door was unlocked so she walked right in. There were 15 other women sitting in the lobby area either on their phone or whispering to each other. Some pieces of furniture still had tarp over them. Suddenly, a sweaty man in a orange short sleeve button down came around the corner.

"Casey! Casey Grant that is here to save our ass for this launch in two months!"

Casey chuckled, putting on her million dollar bubbly personality, "Hey! You must be the manager!"

He coughed heartily and she cringed. "Sorry sweetheart. Don't mind the cough I've had it foreva. I'm Mike Balotelli. Meet your strippers, girls, trainees whatever you call them." He brought his large watch to his face. "I gotta go in the office, Ciao."

As quickly as he entered, he exited, leaving her in the room of women. Some looked older than her and some younger. They looked up at her, the set of eyes telling a different story. Some full of wonder, others apathetic.

Casey smiled as she sat down on the floor with them. "Well if you didn't hear earlier my name is Casey Grant and I'm the executive performance trainer for Grant Enterprises. I'm excited to be here with you all for the next two months to get ready for this launch. First, let's introduce ourselves with our preferred names. This could be a stage name or government, no big deal."

A young lady, probably close to 21, with a petite frame stood up. "Hey everyone! My name is Willow-Mae." She was even shorter than Casey standing at 5ft 3in but full of energy. "I just moved here from Kentucky and I'm sooo glad to be here with yall." She smiled widely at everyone, but some returned her friendliness with a grimace.

They went around the lobby as each woman introduced themselves, Casey nodded and looked at each woman in the eye. She wanted them to know that she had their undivided attention. Even though her business had fallen apart, that didn't mean she had to be rude and take her frustration out on them. It wasn't their fault.

After the introductions, Casey stood up. "So you may or may not know, this training program isn't like at other places. During these two months we will be spending 8 hours together to conditioning and learning routines. This work, the work of a dancer involves using each muscle in your body. Now you don't have to be a professional, just willing to learn. You will learn solo, double and triple choreography together. You will build muscles and feel pain in unknown places. But I promises when we open those doors, you will amaze and astound. In other words take before and after pics." She laughed with a few others in the room. "Who here has dance experience?"

A few women raised their hands, even Willow-Mae.

"Okay who has dance experience, outside of the club scene." Willow was the only one who kept her hand raised. So Casey asked her, "Where did you gain the experience?"

In Willow-Mae's thickest Kentucky accent, she said, "I was a majorette in my high school band. We even performed at the county fair! It was a real hoot. It wasn't a fancy dancey competition, but it is experience!"

Casey nodded along while the other women ignored her. "Well that's great Willow-Mae! I appreciate you sharing." She confidently strode towards the stage platform hopping up towards the main pole, facing the ladies.

"Alright sexy ass BITCHES. Let's get on this stage and start with some warms ups to get the body moving."

The manager had emailed her last week and confirmed that construction for the stage and poles were already up to OSHA regulation so she felt safe using them. As the other women staggered behind her, Casey tapped in to the familiar glow that filled her when she led a class. She turned on her speaker and opened her music app, and played her gym playlist featuring Cardi B and other female rappers.

She demonstrated the stretch then the group joined in replicating it. She walked around the stage, letting them know to pointe their feet or engage their core.

"One thing that's important to me is strength. If you are not strong in the right places, you will fall more often then you want. Yes, a weak core will cause you to fall. It happens, but when you trust the pole and your core strength, that's when you'll grow. On that note, let's start with conditioning."

They did push ups, sit ups and pull ups on the pole. Since there were only 5 poles , she broke them into groups of 3 during conditioning to give some time to relax until the next circuit. By the time they finished for the day, Casey was not looking forward to the trek back to the hotel. The hole of loneliness that had a lack of love. Her prison cell.

As she was packing her bag to leave, Willow-Mae came up to her, "Ma'am that was the hardest workout I've had EVER. We didn't even use weights, have mercy."

"It'll get easier as the weeks go on. You'll look, see and feel the difference in your body just wait."

Her smile grew even wider, her red curls still bounced next to her ears. "I can't wait! See ya tomorrow."

Casey put her fake smile back on and waved. When she

walked out of those doors, that heavy emotional weight resumed it's position on her shoulders. The studio, her home, making rent, losing 2 months of progress, no close family... it was becoming too much at once. What if someone broke into the studio while she was gone. Which reminded her that she needed a security system. *The list keeps growing and growing.* She was alone fending for herself and the dream that now felt a mile away.

A text from Sky came through.

Sky: Hey! Call me asap. I got a friend that helps young business women with business plans, tax stuff, the whole works.

CASEY FROWNED. She would need more than just a little help to get launched.

Me: I don't know. Is it really worth it? I mean, I'm not even in town right now

THEN AN INCOMING CALL from Sky came through and Casey put in her earbud, unwillingly answering as she walked down the street. "Hey girl."

"Let me tell you something. I'm not letting you give up on this. You have a studio; all we need to do is fill in the gaps. Let me help you while you're gone."

Casey sucked her teeth. "You shouldn't have to do that.

This is some bullshit about me being here anyway. I just let my mom down and wasted her money." Her eyes started to burn, not from the bitter cold air, but for her dreams that won't come true even with a miracle.

Sky sighed into the phone, "Casey. I've seen you when you teach. You engage with everyone, make everyone feel welcome. You have really helped women on the journey of loving themselves. You're ready to do your own thing! I keep telling you I'm here to help you. I'm rooting for you! I think we can get this done together."

Casey's mind was spinning. Sky *could* oversee a few things. She would only give her the website password and the building keys. Both were in her bedroom in the top drawer. Even though she's in a situation that she can't control, she had to be adjustable.

"Okay... okay let's do it. You have my spare key so go into my condo and in my dresser on the back wall in the closet is the set of keys to the studio and the website passwords and stuff. I think staff wise, it should just be you and me. We can start small."

"Yes!" A big crash sounded in the background. "Nettie! What was that?"

"Nothing!" Nettie yelled back in the background.

Sky chuckled into the phone. "I'll call my friend and schedule a call with the three of us for the breakdown. We are going to make this happen Casey, no matter what."

Casey nodded to herself, she knew Sky couldn't see it. "I mean us doing this won't guarantee this is a failure. But we can give it a shot, even though I'm states away."

"See stop that, we are going to focus on the positive and what *we* can control. I'll go by your place to pick up the keys and sign into the website account. Maybe I could even give suggestions too? I'll just write them down so we can talk about it together. I promise I won't change anything you've done already."

"That sounds fine."

"Well I'm going to see what your niece broke. I'll talk to you later. Call me if anything comes up."

Casey chuckled as a cold breeze hit her cheek. "Alright don't be too harsh."

"Uh huh." They laughed while disconnecting the line.

When Casey opened her hotel room door and threw her stuff down as she kicked her shoes off, she thought that maybe, just maybe. The world wasn't ending.

She still couldn't bring herself to call Denver again. But that was a different problem for a different day.

First, her business. Then, her love life. He would wait for her. Right?

AS CASEY WAS MAKING her bed, she answered the incoming call from Gemini. "Wassup bitch."

"Nothing much hoe just livin the fiancé life." They laughed. It felt good to hear Gemini's voice. Casey loved how their relationship grew. "I called because one, I miss you and two, I can't wait for this Bachelorette party! Serena said you and her planned something a while ago. What are you guys gonna do?"

Casey's heart cheered, that Gemini was excited because she definitely deserved to be. " Not telling! It's a secret but you'll have fun. You'll FaceTime me when you pick out your dress right?"

"Of course! How was the first practice? I know it was last week but still wanna know what's goin on."

"This is a good group and they're pretty cool. I'm cleaning

up this room before I head to this hookah lounge to meet them. They are picking up the moves fast so I don't doubt they'll be ready."

"And they have an awesome teacher."

Casey smiled to herself. "You're giving me way too much right now."

"Nuh uh! You are a bad bitch, okay? Cause there is no way I would be able to get as high up on a pole as you can then land in a fucking split. Then look good. I would have a concussion."

They laughed harder, almost falling over. "Shut the fuck up! That's why I teach, it's just a mindset and practice."

"Mmhm I'll be signing up as soon as classes drop. You already know!"

Casey started arranging her outfits. "I'll let you know when the site is live."

"What are you getting into tonight?"

"Some of the other girls wanted to hang out tonight and go to a Hookah lounge. They begged me so I'm going too."

"They had to beg you? You usually don't turn away from a party."

Casey sighed. "Yea I guess. I'm still disappointed about this studio. But me, Sky and one of her friends had a good talk about taxes and stuff. Sky and I are partners now which has helped A LOT. But what if the place burns down? What if someone gets hurt?"

"That's what insurance and liability forms are for." Gemini said playfully. "You have to protect yourself and your business. What's the name of it again?"

"The Passion Pole Studio."

"PPS, mmm I like it. I can see the name in lights now. Just keep pushing and don't take the hard lessons for granted."

She nodded to herself. "Your right. Well I need to get dressed so I'll talk to you later. Love you."

"Love you sis!"

AT THE LOUNGE, Casey was comfortable and it wasn't crowded. Willow Mae was getting ahead of herself on the drinks, but everyone else was pretty chill. After the 3rd round of shots, Willow-Mae was definitely getting more drunk because she kept telling stories. "Did you know my parents made love under a Willow tree? That's how they named me. Isn't that gross?"

A Migos song plays and the excitement in the room builds. "Damn Takeoff is really gone." Casey says mournfully. "Talk about a death that fucked the city up."

Another woman named Princess chuckled, "You're so Atlanta. But that whole situation was messed up."

Casey shook her head. "I guess we all have to 'walk it like we talk it'."

Princess turned at looked at Casey. "That was corney as hell but funny."

She shrugged and smiled, hoping that Denver would've appreciated the joke, too. After coming back to the hotel and taking a shower, she patted her face dry to begin her nightly skin care routine. As she put on her overnight moisturizer, she thought about what Denver was doing this time of night. She hadn't reached out to him and he hadn't called her. She ran out the chances she wasted.

DENVER WALKED into Helping Human Helpers headquarters. He had a meeting with the contract manager to find out if he'll be working with them one more year. The office was on the top floor with a view of the North Georgia mountains. It felt weird for him to be in Atlanta and Casey not be. He wished she was there. He wished she'd call because he was tired of chasing her. For now it was back to reality.

"So Brian, we've received feedback from your last few engagements and they haven't gone so well as your others. Can you tell me more about that?"

He took a deep breath. "I know at the conference in Washington I started crying on stage. I saw someone in a pink shirt and I thought... but that is no excuse."

The brunette-haired women arched her eyebrow. "Well based on what we heard, we think you need a break from assignments. We're suspending your contract for 30 days. We understand the strain of traveling so this is some time off for your... wellness. It's a good break to focus on yourself."

Fuck it's that bad. "Will I get paid?"

She looked towards her computer and back at him. "Unfortunately no. We'll reach out to you at the end of the 30 days for an update."

Then there was silence. He guessed that was the end of that. "I guess I'll go and await the call. Thanks so much."

When he made it back to the hotel, we wrote down a few video ideas for his OnlyFans account to make his money back. He always had savings to cover for at least two months so he would survive, just no more traveling.

No grand trip to New York to win back the woman he loved.

CHAPTER 23
ONE MONTH LATER

CASEY HAS BEEN WORKING to turn her situation to a
positive. While in New York she had the meeting to set up her
tax forms for the studio this year and FaceTimed with Sky
while she was at the studio to share content, website and flyer
ideas.

With Sky now being a teacher/partner, she was been
creating a buzz about the studio, too. She was making posts
three times a week across her social media platforms. Casey
also didn't stop with her content. She made a post about Sky
officially joining and being away on assignment. But the launch
date would be releasing soon. Instead of getting her usual 50
likes, that post got 300.

She needed to finished the website soon.

Casey greeted everyone as she came into the studio. "Hey
y'all!"

"Hey Case! I've been trying to figure out the Ballerina
move you showed yesterday. You hop on like this right?"

Casey watched her wrap her hand around the pole the

wrong way for the move. "Willow-Mae! Wait wait! Before you try that move, put your hands here and here."

The young trainee placed her hands in proper place coping as Casey instructed. "Pull from your core and really lift! While also relaxing your face, it's about feeling light but being strong while looking sexy."

Willow-Mae tried to shake the unsure look from her face. She tried the move again, but lost the grip on her left hand. She hit the ground, hard. A loud plop rang around the room. "Golly gee! My stars, if I don't nail this move just go right ahead and put a possum in my casket."

Everyone looked at her, giggles rising. "Huh? What?"

Then Casey added, "Now if Willow-Mae wants a possum, raccoon or squirrel in her casket that's up to her and nobody else." She tried to hide her laugh. "That's doesn't mean you can laugh."

"Oh it's fine Casey. It's just one of those thangs my mama would say when she was frustrated." She said with a shrug. "I will condition more and try it again. But I'm nailing it before you leave missy."

Casey poured the pole grip on her palms. "Now this move is not easy. So don't force yourself. It's called the ballerina because it's beautiful and difficult. There are technically multiple ways to enter this move. So I'll only show two."

She leaped and grabbed the pole aimlessly, swirling her right leg around. Then she hooked both legs in front of her while her arm was behind her. Then she regrabbed the pole with her right hand and slowed down her speed and took a deep breath. "So that is the advanced way. The easier way is to sit and hook your inside leg." She took two steps and swung her left leg around to build momentum and displayed sitting, and the hook and hand placement.

"Ahh, I see what you were saying about my hands now. I'll work on it!" Willow-Mae said excitedly drenched in sweat.

The other performers practiced behind her, some were already nailing the advanced way perfectly while others completed bits and pieces. This move was her favorite because it really showed her muscle definition. The sports bra and shorts she was wearing made her look even more beautiful while displaying her core, her skin, her hair. She spun a few more times and freestyled, feeling the pull in her back when she grabbed her foot behind her head and her front leg extended. She was upside down with her leg extended, foot pointed, then she gracefully hopped down to everyone amazed and applauding.

A trainees voice in the back said, "Now if I had some money, I would throw it for that last move. It makes your pussy pop." All the women roared in laughter.

The comment was the perfect ending for their technical practice. She was feeling good and trusted the performers to stay if they needed it. Almost everyone left along with Casey, except for Willow-Mae as she gave a determined look to the pole.

WHILE CASEY WAS TAKING her clothes out of the hotel dryer, Ayden called her.

"Damn so you just dropped a nigga? Where you at?"

She sighed. "I'm in Manhattan, *nigga*." She said frustrated. "I've actually been here."

"You couldn't let me know?"

"Nah cause you don't answer when I call remember?"

He sucked his teeth. "Damn I don't drop everything and run to you like pretty boy and your trippin? That's crazy."

"I don't think it's crazy. We're just friends A. We just fuck around. When I'm with him, I'm not reminded of having to pin up some neighborhood kids for jumpin yo ass."

He was quiet on the other end. She picked up her bag and went to the elevator.

He finally spoke. "I know the situation I put you in sucked. Sorry. I didn't mean for that to happen."

"But it did. So what do you want me to do?"

He sighed. "Nothing. You don't need to worry about. I handled it. That's what I called to tell you."

"What the fuck do you mean, you handled it."

"I spoke to your dad. He said he'd make a call. Well, he told me to make a call."

"YOU DID WHAT! Oh hell no. Get off my line. This is why I don't fuck with this shit. Now you just made things worse! Bye!"

Her hands started shaking as the doors closed. Thankfully she was alone. Her vibrating palm began to sweat as she selected her number for her floor. Her other arm squeezing the life out of the bag. She took a deep breath as she stepped out of the elevator, just in case someone was outside. When she made it back to her room, she quickly got in and closed the door behind her.

Then her heart broke. Why was Ayden trying to make the situation even worse? She put her hands to her head and slid down to the ground. Her back leaning on the door. "Fuck that was so stupid!" She didn't want to see another news coverage of another death in her hometown all because her father made a move. A drive by. A home invasion with no survivors. It was always something. Her entire body seemed to be on a different frequency while her heart was racing.

"Fucking shit fuck." *Don't lose it. Don't lose it. What do you see?* She looked at her pink suitcase with rounded dark pink shapes. Then she started to count them, each number slowly to calm herself. Now she had to call the only other person who could help. She took out her phone and dialed.

She answered on the first ring. "You rarely call me first. This must be really bad."

The sound of Coraline's voice was calming but also annoying. "Yea it's bad Ayden called Bull, and went to see him. He did something."

She heard the phone drop and Coraline scramble to pick up the phone. "I'm sorry. I thought you said Bull and uh, I can't think about that right now. Unless if you really said Bull, as in your father."

She sighed. "Yes the murderous cocaine slinging Bull has been let loose."

Then Casey rambled everything that took place on New Year's with tears in her eyes. She felt better finally telling her big sister what happened, but she also knew it would stress her out.

Coraline's phone hit the floor again after she finished. She yet again scrambled. "Shit. Fuck this is going to be expensive. Okay now I have to fucking go down there. SHIT. Okay it's fine. Don't you stress about it. I got it. You're safe either way since you're not here, whether you know that or not. I'll talk to you later. DAMNIT."

Then the line was silent. Call ended. She didn't want to tell Coraline what happened. But now it was a whole thing.

The next morning Casey called out of work for the first time all year. She would have made herself work through it, but she didn't have the energy. Her mind was not focused; she didn't want to move or be seen. She laid on the hotel couch, scrolling through her contacts. Who could she call here? Dick was a great way to keep your mind off of things. Then Nick NYC came on the screen.

She called and quickly hung up to make it seem like an accident.

Nick NYC: Hey! Sorry I missed your call. You in town? Want to link up?

Casey: Sure I've got some time today

Nick NYC: *send address* let's meet here at 4pm

Casey: See you there

SHE WALKED into the lounge right on time. It was around the corner from her hotel so it wasn't a horrible walk. Other than the horrible smell of all the piled trash on the sidewalk. The lounge was full of empty seats, but people were slowly starting to come in. She looked around the room and recognized Nick as soon as their met eyes. He was dark chocolate wearing a light grey suit. He smiled as he crossed the lounge with his drink in hand. "Hey Casey! You look amazing as always."

Even though she didn't feel like it, she said, "Thank you."

"What can I get you? The menu and drinks here are pretty nice."

"I'll just have a glass of water and Ceaser salad with grilled chicken." She said with a weak smile. He waved the waiter over and let him know.

Once they walked away his eyebrow arched, "What's wrong? You're usually bubbly or want a shot."

She sighed, "I got a lot going on right now. This is probably the first assignment I wasn't excited to travel for."

"Woah is Casey Grant ready to settle down? The girl I know would've talked to at least three people by now and fucked at least one."

"Shut up. There's nothing wrong with wanting to settle. Has someone actually kept your attention?" she asked, raising her eyebrow.

He twisted his lips, "We aren't talking about me though. So... who or what has got a hold on you like that?"

"Someone and something."

He made a motion for her to continue as he sipped his drink.

"There is this... guy that I am growing feelings for. But he wants something more serious and I don't. At least I don't think I do. And, I'm working on opening my own pole studio and it's not as easy as I thought it would be."

Nick nodded, "What's not so easy about it? There's nothing bad about being serious with somebody. You don't have to fight it, if you think you found it."

"Usually I just record my videos or follow the prompt I made for my trainings. But now I have to think about really bringing in consistent money, keep the lights on and trying to get people to come to classes and keeping the studio clean and so much more. It's getting to be too overwhelming."

Nick took out his phone and started scrolling and typing.

"Wow I said all that and you just hop on your phone?"

"I'm asking a friend for something to see if she can help with something else."

Casey folded her arms, "Right." She noticed the ring on his finger, "Wait you're married now?" She almost screamed.

He laughed. "Yes I am engaged and out of the game."

"If you're engaged, why did you agree to meet me?"

He shrugged, "I never said we would fuck and we're at a public place. I also know your call and hang up routine so I wanted to entertain you for awhile." They laughed as her water and salad arrived. "So it still seems like there is something at the back of your mind. What else is going on with you? I know we haven't kicked it in awhile but." He shrugged. "I'm here now so break it down for me. Why are you hesitating with him? Can he not fuck?"

She had a flashback of Denver blindfolded and handcuffed under her. "No, we definatelty have sexual chemistry. He's flown out multiple times to see me. He's just... fucking perfect. He has the perfect family, the perfect home to grow up in. He invited me to spend Christmas with him and I said yes."

Nick coughed. "A holiday? Away from your folks? Oh you like him forreal."

She made a throaty growl. "Tuh! Like he's actually cool with his dad and talks to him. He listens to great music, forgives me after I keep showing my ass. I think I lost him for good. That is stressing me the fuck out."

Nick nodded.

"But I texted you because I just wanted some dick that's all. You know me. I'm just bored," she said shrugging her shoulders.

"Do I need to put on my psychologist hat? Don't forget I'm a professor in Psychology and you know I'm a trained counselor."

Casey stared at the salad, waiting to speak. Something moved the corner of her eye but when she looked nobody was there. Then she stared at the front door to the restaurant.

The door. The door.

"It's okay, you can tell me, Casey. What's been going on with you?"

She took a deep breath and pressed her lips together. "On the New Year day, I was hanging with another friend of mine, and his place got ran into. I had to point a gun at a couple of the niggas. I knew who they were too. I know my way around a gun, but I never wanted to use it on a person, you know? Especially a black man. But I had to protect my friend, you know? It's not fair to jump people in their own house just to prove a point."

Nick gulped his drink. "Did you have to use it?"

She shook her head. "No I just pointed it. But I was prepared to. I had to do something." An unexpected tear fell from her eye. "I've been paranoid ever since."

"They must have been bold. They couldn't have known you were there. You're protected everywhere you go; with who your dad is and all."

She twirled her glass of water with the straw. "Yea, but the rules are different now, I guess. I just keep ignoring the feeling."

He nodded, "I understand. I stopped a guy on the subway for grabbing a random girl's ass. She was just a fucking kid. He didn't realize I saw him. There are some messed up people in the world and healing looks different for everyone. That was an assault on you and your friend's personal space. You should do what ever you need to to heal. If that means putting a chair in front of the door, do it. If that means carrying a taser in your pocket, do it. Do whatever you need to feel safe and you'll slowly come back to yourself."

She never thought about it like that. "Thank you Nick," she stood up and hugged his slim shoulders. *Damn I wanted him to break my back in.* "Your fiancé is a lucky girl."

A smile spread wide across his face. "I know and I'll never meet another person like her. She's really sweet. She works at NYU too. I need to claim her before she changes her mind." He laughed. "Sometimes you just, know."

Denver knew about her, but maybe he was wrong.

She walked out onto the sidewalk and her phone rang with Coraline's picture taking over her phone screen. She answered. "Hey Coraline," she said plainly, walking back to the hotel.

"Heeey," Coraline said with a salesmen smile. "How is my sister doing in NYC so far? The manager said he's impressed from how much better the performers, are doing already. Great job! Even though you did call out today."

"Gee thanks."

Coraline was silent on the other end, waiting for more. "There must be more on your mind than what we talked about yesterday. You can tell me, I'm wearing my sister hat now."

Casey took a deep breath. "I miss Denver."

"He can't come up and visit? He's flown to Atlanta a few times for you, right?"

"Maybe but he's mad at me."

"For what?"

Casey sighed harder, "Ayden."

Coraline was quiet again. "That's when this whole thing really started. On your birthday, am I right? I thought I saw him."

"Yea, you were just very distracted so I couldn't really tell you then huh."

"Shut up. Why are you even still giving him the time of day? He brought a lot of attention to you. What if you got hurt? What if those stupid fucks didn't know who you were?"

Casey stomped her foot on the pavement. "I wanted him okay?! I want him! I want Denver! I want everyone! Fuck! Now I'm literally in a party city sad as fuck because neither of them are here. Denver is mad at me, I don't want Ayden. I'm fucking lonely."

A tear fell from her eye. The people that passed her ignored her and she was thankful as she continued walking. "I'm tired of this hotel room, but I don't want to go anywhere else. What's the point?"

"I know the feeling of loneliness well sis. But, to me, it sounds like your trying to fill a hole with people. Now, it's okay to do that. But you can't control them. You can't make Denver talk to you or Ayden drop everything to run to you. You have to fill your own hole. When was the last time you had fun without either of them there?"

Casey thought about it for awhile. Fun without them? Maybe the paint and sip she went to with Gemini. Even though a man was there, it was still a fun experience. "I went to this painting thing was Gemini and it was my first time going to an... event like that. I had a great time and a lot of fun. I also went out with some girls here and laughed a little."

"Good! You have to search for those moments too Casey. Alone. It's all good to fuck around when you want to. But it's your *why*. You have to pour into yourself. Have you even gotten your nails done while being there?"

She sniffled. "No."

Coraline gasped. "Oh this is worse than I thought. Do I need to come out there?"

Here she goes, that would only make her stress worse. In a 'I love my sister but she doesn't have to come right now' kind of way. Casey felt closer to Calvin than her anyway. But never hated her. "It's not that deep! I'll make a nail appointment this week or something. I'll look for some fun. Maybe visit a library or something."

"Yes! Support local libraries! Go to a museum or something. I'm giving you the rest of the week off, with permission."

Casey looked at the phone, then brought it back to her ear. "This is Coraline Workaholic Grant right? It's Tuesday."

"Yea I know. I also know when you're calling out for help. So take the week, love on you, and do something new. If you want to come back home and leave the project early, I can send a replacement."

Casey started coughing. A replacement? Who else would teach the performers pole work *her* way? But, she did need a break. "Now I really know I'm not talking to my big sister. But I will take you up on that. I'll call you on Saturday with my stay or go plans."

"Sounds good. You can text me in between too, you know."

"Yea yea I know. Big sis saving the day again."

Coraline laughed. "Isn't that my job? I wore this badge so y'all could do what you wanted. Everyone sacrifices... I'm going to send you a gift since you don't want me to come. Don't worry about anything."

"Aye aye captain Grant."

"You are such a head ass Casey. Have fun this week."

"You too, I love you!"

"I love you too little sis, goodnight."

TO DO list for the rest of the week.

1. Do whatever I need to do to feel safe again
2. Rest and relax

THAT SHOULDN'T BE TOO *hard right?*

CHAPTER 24

CASEY STARTED her Wednesday with a complete Spa
package at the hotel. They did a scalp treatment, deep tissue
massage, pedicure and manicure. When she walked out, she
had new skin and a new relaxed body. She hoped she didn't
snore during the massage because that was the best nap she's
had in awhile. No nightmare that time.

When she made it back to her room, she took a few selfies
in her hotel bathroom with a smize. Her natural curls bouncing
in the mirror. Too bad she had nobody to send them too. *That's
fine, I took the pictures for me to enjoy.*

Coraline Big Sis: What have you been up to
today?

Casey: Spa day with the works, hair take
down and wash, mani, pedi. New skin
who dis

Coraline: lol What happened to sight seeing?

Casey: I don't wanna. Fuck the world

THERE WAS a soft knock on Casey's door. Her body froze. She grabbed her taser from the nightstand, then buzzed it. *Yep charged.* Then quietly approached the door.

Coraline: I sent you something you might enjoy

SHE LOOKED through the peep hole. It was Calvin! She jumped up, squealed and threw the door open. "Calvin! Oh my gosh you came!"

"We needed a wedding planning break." Gemini said around the corner.

Casey tackled them into a hug, pulling them into her room. "Ahh shit!" She hugged them both tighter. "You don't know how happy I am to see y'all. Why do you need a wedding planning break?" She turned the taser off and threw it in a corner before they noticed.

Gemini rolled her eyes as they got comfy in her room. "We can't decide on a cake flavor. I want lemon and he wants German chocolate. You know what your brother said? He wants a Groom's cake. Have you ever heard of a groom's cake? You know my aunt raised me and she's never been married. I never really knew my parents like that and they were never married so I don't even know who to ask. We're 60 days away from the wedding and your hard headed brother pulled this. More things to add on the list to think about." She sighed and wiped her hand down her face. "But were not talking about us." She pressed her hand to her temple. "We are here for you, girl."

Casey laughed. Calvin made himself comfortable on the sectional, pulling a book out of his bag. Then she remembered she was texting Coraline.

> Casey: Calvin and Gemini are here! Was this the surprise?

> Coraline: Your welcome lol have fun!

"HOW LONG WILL y'all be here?" Casey asked as Gemini sat in the chair by the window.

"I wish forever, but we fly back Sunday afternoon."

Calvin chimed in, "Yea I need to finalize the summer schedule again with everyone since the kids will be out of school next month and the wedding and honeymoon are a month after that."

"Where are you going for the honeymoon?"

Gemini looked out the window and down the city lights. "Jamaica! I can't wait to sit on the beach, put my feet in the water and have people call me 'The New Mrs. Grant.' I ordered a white bikini and everything. That's one of the few things I'm looking forward to." Calvin smiled at his book. "Also, don't think I know when you're deflecting. We need to talk. Walk me down to the lobby." Gemini moved from the floor to ceiling windows and Casey locked arms with her as they left the room.

"DO you think Calvin noticed that we left?" Casey asked as they sat at the bar. A strawberry daiquiri for Gemini and two tequila shots for Casey.

"I doubt it. You know he goes deaf when that book is open. But I can't talk bad about him because I do the same thing. Are we the first people to visit you since you've been here?" she asked bouncing her eyebrows.

"Yea actually. You're the first people to see my hotel room besides housekeeping."

Gemini did a fake gasp. "Not a dry spell! Got the rose working overtime. What about Denver and Ayden?"

"Nope." Casey shrugged. "Denver is tired of my shit."

"I don't blame him."

Casey chuckled. "I was kind of mean on my birthday. Well our birthday."

"Kind of? Our birthday? Of course y'all are birthday twins. Damn scorpios. He got stood up in front of the whole club. We all saw you hand him your keys. I was like *damnn*. But I didn't want to say too too much because I don't judge you. I'm reckless too sometimes."

Her eyes widened. "Please tell me your joking. That many people weren't looking right?"

"Y'all kissed after being in the building for like 2 minutes, he was sitting in our section AND you were the birthday girl. Yes people saw that and were watching you." Gemini leaned closer to her. "I don't blame you, other dude was fine. And you are single so do your shit."

Casey couldn't keep ignoring the situation. "Yea Ayden

kinda of put me in a messed up position on New Year, but we're at least on speaking terms now, I guess. Denver?" She paused. "I used up all my forgiveness cards. Then when I called him another bitch was there. I haven't reached out to him since."

Gemini looked at her confused. "Why did you stop talking to him? Did he call you in between on some disrespectful stuff?"

She shook her head no. "I was just mad and jealous that he was with somebody else. He said he loved me and I didn't say it back. But I can't be mad right? But I don't want to tell him that. And I miss him. I miss his fucking family. I even brought the robe with me. I just want to feel close to him. Not because seeing someone else made me jealous, really, but it made it realize how cool he actually is. The way his heartbeat calms me down after a long day. It made me remember all the times we have laughed together. I can't watch him be with someone else. We're supposed to be together. I do love him."

"So what are you going to do? Are you going to show him how much he means to you? They like feeling like the person they care for, wants them back."

Casey scoffed and slowly started to laugh with Gemini. "I need to do something. Wait. I'm over here talking about these guys and haven't checked in on you. Are you ready to be *married*? The Grant family isn't like everyone else."

Gemini chuckled. "Yes! I love you, Coraline, y'alls Mom. It's not the after I'm worried about, I'm more worried about the day of. I just want everything to be perfect. But I'm having decision fatigue. Like why do I have to pick where people sit? Just pick a seat." she laughed. "I'm almost ready to go to the courthouse and jump the broom. When Coraline was worried about you and reached out to us, I was glad I could put an itinerary together for us to go around. It gave me something else to think about and I missed you."

They pulled each other in for a hug.

"So you really made an itinerary, how long did it take?"

Gemini pulled a teal colored book out of her purse, then held up a folded up piece of paper. "Ta da! I wanted to keep it in a safe space. I worked on it on the way here and I have a back up copy on my phone."

"As your bookmark?"

She shrugged, "Yes, anyways. So, on Thursday and Friday be ready to walk and move around. Our first stop is Schomburg Center for Research in Black Culture, they have an exhibit on Langston Hughes that you will love. I hope."

Casey's heart warmed, "Really? I didn't know."

"Yea it's with the public library so you know that was where I checked first."

"I can't wait".

THE NEXT DAY, they visit the Langston Hughes exhibit and were blown away. "These photos were taken decades ago and they are still around." Casey whispered wanting to touch one.

"Yea," Gemini agreed looking behind her. "The Harlem poem always gets to me. I just might reread *A Raisin in the Sun.*"

Calvin was across the room, speaking to the other librarians.

When they left, they sat down at a diner themed restaurant and Calvin lightly nudged Casey shoulder. "It's so good to see you. I missed you, sis. I go by your place every now and then to make sure it's okay and it is."

She exhaled. "Good. I was in my head so much I forgot to

ask you to. Sky has been by there frequently too so that's helped me bring more peace."

"No big deal. I'll always look out for you. So how is studio planning going? You haven't quit yet, right?"

She shook her head no. "Sky is helping me so much. I literally wouldn't have hung on this long without her help and connections. We're going 50/50. She's just as passionate as me and believes in the vision too."

Gemini beamed looking at her. "I can't wait! Everything is going to go so smooth. We are here for you either way. I'm so proud of how far you've come."

"Oh my gosh don't say that. I haven't even done anything."

"Yes you have!" Calvin and Gemini say in unison. Then her brother continued, "I watched you clean and check in. The posts you were making that said coming soon. Everyone has to start somewhere. You're setting the building blocks now. Just like how I had to with the library. When the foundation is strong, the building is stronger and last longer."

Casey scooted out of her seat and hugged Calvin. He always knew exactly what to say. Then she hugged Gemini shaking her side to side. "What would I do without you guys?"

"Be depressed and lonely."

"Most likely."

FRIDAY MORNING they went to breakfast and walked around Central Park. Gemini kept taking pictures of 'hot spots' from "Law and Order: SVU" and "ELF". Although Calvin had an earbud in his ear of an audiobook, he was still talking to them. When they walked, Casey locked arms with Gemini and leaned her head on her shoulder. She leaned her head on top of hers. She hoped she knew she grew another sister. There was something about the red clay of Georgia that she missed. New York had traffic, but Atlanta's traffic gave a great view, too.

When they were sitting in the hotel lobby that night, a man in a grey suit offered to buy her a drink. She turned him down to Gemini's surprise. "Oh, so you really down bad for Denver."

Casey put her hand to her temple. "Very bad. I fucking hate it."

"And you haven't called him because why?"

"Because why would he want to talk to me? I didn't tell you this but I left a nasty voice message. Like embarrassingly mean voice message. I would hate me if I got a message like that."

Gemini gave her a sympathetic glance. "Look take it from me. You may not want to hear what he has to say but give him a chance. He needs the space to open up to you about how he's feeling. Just like how you need to apologize for hurting him. And like a real apology. So stop fighting this feeling. And sis, if your waiting for him to fly out here first, he isn't."

"Damn you had to put me together like that?"

Gemini gave her a look. "Yes bitch, cause you're acting stupid." They laughed together and hugged each other tightly. Casey would call him to apologize, but how? What could she say or do to let him know she really cared about him.

The next morning, Casey came to the realization that Calvin and Gemini would be leaving sooner than she wanted them to. When Sunday came she was tried to pull herself back together. Saying goodbye to them was hard enough. She was finally able to have fun and not be as paranoid. She was around genuine love.

"I want to come home, send someone else to finish. The pole studio is launching this summer and I need to make that my priority," she told Coraline.

Coraline chuckled. "I knew you would. Your replacement

has been training at the club while you've been on vacation. I'll email you your ticket to leave tomorrow, so start packing."

"Actually, can you have my one way ticket go to Denver, Colorado? I'll pay my way home from there."

She could hear Coraline giggle on the phone. A real *haunting* giggle.

"Sure," she said back in her professional tone. "I'll see you when you come back to work."

CHAPTER 25

HE SAT ON HIS BED, staring at his ceiling fan, wishing he never met the tornado that was Casey Grant. Why did she have to wink at him from across the room at that retreat? She knew she had everyone's attention. Why did she have to be so fucking sexy and independent?

Fuck it.

He opened his photos album and opened his 'Casey 😘' Album. He then stared at the FaceTime photo of her blowing a kiss. Those sexy ass pouty lips. Those lips he missed.

I want a girlfriend, a real girlfriend that really wants me, for me. That's what I deserve.

In his heart, he knew Casey cared about him. Even if it hadn't been spoken. He went a year without talking to her and still thought about her everyday some way or form.

How long would he have to wait this time?

A second later his phone rang, her beautiful face on his screen. He stopped himself from answering quickly but he answered on the last ring. "Hello?"

"Hey Denver, er Brian. Whatever you want me to call you. How are you?"

"I'm managing." He was a wreck and a mess. "How are you?"

"I'm actually not doing well."

He sat up. "And why is that?"

"I miss you. Like really miss you."

Then there was silence on the line. "I miss you too. But I'm not blowing more money to see you and be ignored. It's not worth it anymore."

"I know. I know. That's why I'm not asking you to do that. I was actually going to ask if I could come see you."

See me? "Wait you'd fly out here, to Colorado, to see me?"

"Yea I've never done that for you before. But you've done it for me plenty of times. I need to see you. I need to talk... and apologize for a lot of things."

He moved some papers around in the background. He'd drop everything for her but he didn't want to seem like the puppy he was. "I should be able to move somethings around. I'll text you my address."

"I'll send you my flight information. I can't wait."

"I will admit I am looking forward to seeing you and hearing what you have to say," he said truthfully.

She was making the effort to see him. She was trying to see him after weeks. *I guess I didn't have to wait much longer.*

HE STOOD outside his car staring at his watch, then a pink cloud moved in the corner of his eye. When he looked to the left, he saw the love of his life in a bubblegum pink pullover, a black skirt and heels, with the straight middle part her hair flowing to her waist. He had to stop himself from running to her. He couldn't make it too easy.

She hesitantly approached him, pulling her suitcase behind her. "Hi," she said with a small smile.

"Hey," he said as seriously as he could.

Then she opened her arms and wrapped him around his neck as he nuzzled his nose into her jacket. "I missed this," she whispered. "You were so patient. Even when I wasn't patient with myself. I'm truly sorry for hurting you. Especially on our birthday. I could've communicated better with you about my past. The pain I was feeling, I was taking it out on you and you didn't deserve that."

He squeezed her tighter. "I missed you too. I thought I lost you again. But I was willing to wait for you." They held each other for so long the cars around them started to honk. Then he kissed her and quickly put her luggage in the car.

They made it to his two-story modern built house and she was surprised of the size and how clean it was. "Your house is literally triple the size of my condo. But you still came to visit me?"

"When I asked you to come back with me, you said no." he laughed.

"Denver, I only knew you for three days at that time. I am not Cinderella." They laughed even harder.

It looked like a family home, not the bachelor pad apartment she envisioned he had. "So you're a homeowner?"

"Yea, I thought I told you?"

She shook her head. "Nope you kept that from me."

She walked into the kitchen, and saw four tripods pointed in various positions. One facing the stove, the sink and the counter. Then one on the floor pointing straight up. "You wanna explain all this equipment?"

His face turned bright red as he turned to her. "Oh that's for uh, a side gig."

She gave a deadpan stare. "A side gig."

"Mmhm. I shoot videos."

She observed the kitchen and looked back at him. "Like for TikTok? These are a lot of cameras for that, right? A tripod on the floor?"

He sighed rubbing his head. "Okay, since we're telling our truths, um, they are for videos but for OnlyFans. I'm usually nude."

Her jaw dropped, "So you're telling me that other people pay to see you naked in your house. No wonder why you looked so 'perfect' when we FaceTimed. Cause you know your angles." She sized him up. "How many subscribers and why didn't you tell me?"

He shrugged. "Not a lot, just a little over 55,000 and I don't know why I didn't tell you. But now you know. It's my back up income when I don't get steady gigs with my contract."

She nodded her head. "I'm not mad or anything. But I'd love to see a video." He exhaled like she took 50 pounds off of his chest. Then she opened her arms for a hug.

"Aww shucks for me?" He said mimicking a cartoon character.

"Don't ruin it just come here."

The right side of his lips lifted as he took steps towards her, giving her a light kiss on the cheek and hugged her tighter. They took a deep breath together as he kissed her hair.

"I really missed you Case. But I also wanted to make sure you actually wanted me, not a warm body."

She looked up at him, "I do. I really do. Thank you for supporting me and everything." When she showered and brushed her teeth, she walked into his bedroom and laid her head on him, feeling his heartbeat made her calm. Cozy. Warm.

Home.

She nodded her head, rubbing her cheeks against his shirt. "Casey?"

"Hmm," she hummed wrapping her arms around him squeezing.

"I'm making love to you tonight."

She sat up, "Make love to me? All the times we've had sex doesn't count?"

He shook his head, "Nope. That wasn't love yet. We love each other now right?"

She rolled her eyes as she propped herself on her elbow. "Yes, although it took me awhile."

"And I've always known." He kissed her shoulder then got out the bed. "Can I run you a bath?"

"I just took a shower though."

"I have another bathroom with a soaking tub. I'd love to prepare it for you. I think you would like the view from there."

He got up from the bed.

She sighed and then smiled, "If you say so."

"I won't take long."

When Denver returned, he gently held her hand and brought her to the bathroom. It really could've been a room by itself. "This room has the best view, so I decided to make this the bigger bathroom in the house."

The view opened to endless mountain ranges and a field, a setting resting behind them creating the perfect golden hour.

Casey took off Denver's T-shirt and got in the rose pedaled, bubbly tub. She nodded to the music as "So Fine" by Mint Condition started playing on his speaker. He slowly grabbed her wet foot and began to massage it, his thumb pressing into her skin and going up her calves. Casey groaned as she laid her head back on the waterproof pillow. The water moving slightly "This doesn't look like love making to me, Denver."

He chuckled, "Just because I said I'd make love to you, doesn't mean I'm rushing to the bedroom. There's more ways to make love than sex." Then he sang *so fineeee* to himself as he kissed her left knee, then the right. Inching his way up her body with butterfly kisses. She wiggled her toes in response opening space for him in the tub.

"Come here," she whispered teasingly moving her toes. "The water is fine." He slowly undressed and got in with her.

Even with him in this tub, they had enough room. Without uttering a word, she climbed onto his lap, creating waves that crashed onto the floor. She moved her hips with the suds, kissing the soap off his neck. His hands kept her waist steady as he met her, bounce by bounce. He met each hip rotation, surprising her as he forced her to take all of him. The candle flames bending and grinding with them. When her groan came from her lips, he caught it with a kiss, splashing the water over her arms and shoulders. He held in his love, the best he could. Watching Casey's faces and bouncing breasts took him into a trance.

When the ecstasy washed over her face, he knew it was only the beginning for them. He slowly got out of the tub and grabbed their towels from the towel warmer in the far corner. She smiled, when she covered herself. He wrapped his towel around his waist. He got on one knee and placed pink slippers on her feet. Another look of appreciation filled her face. As they walked back to his bedroom, hand in hand, she took off her towel and got under the cover. Denver slowly joined her after taking his off. She instantly wrapped her arms around his shoulders as he kissed her neck.

"I love you," he breathed.

"I love you too," Casey whispered as her fingertips pressed into his shoulder blades. "What do you taste when you kiss my body?" she asked.

He kissed her jaw, "I taste strength." He kissed the side of her neck, down her clavicle. Then licking her nipples, "Perseverance." He kissed her belly, "Beauty." He kissed around her thighs, blessing the dark spots and stretch marks in between. "This right here is my favorite taste." He palmed her stomach and lifted her lips with his index finger and thumb while he slowly licked her center. "Excellence," he whispered against her quivering lips. He slowly and purposely devoured her core as she ran her fingers through his curls.

"Fuck Denver."

He lifted his head, "No. You know the name I want to hear." He slipped two fingers into her waterfall. She gasped arching her back and meeting his eyes. "Say it like a good girl." As he went faster and faster.

"Bri- Brian baby Brian shit."

He slowed back down, "Good baby." Her head moved towards his dick. "No this is about you."

She sighed even louder when his two fingers tease and plunge her insides. "It's all about you," he whispered before going back to his job.

"Kiss me."

He slowly lifted his head as her fingertips brushed his ears to play in his scalp. Casey lifted her head to meet his lips. Her hands in his curls, his fingers inside of her not letting her go. They both focused on their kisses, their tongues dancing while their chest met. She kept trying to pull him closer and he understood. Without any help, he thrusted his hips slowly to fill her with all he hand.

"Brian, oh faster."

"No I want you to think about my strokes. Think about the man in your arms." He kissed the corner of her mouth. "I want you to relax." Then he brushed his thumbs against her erect nipples before bringing one into his mouth. Casey groaned louder than she thought as her hips buckled, meeting his intention.

"Yes... yes. Put your fingers in my mouth." His finger fresh with the taste of her met her mouth as she sucked him. A look crossed over his eyes as he watched her and it made her come on sight.

"Fuck! This is my pussy."

"It's all fucking yours." He turned her to the side and lifted her leg as he continued. One hand was on her leg, as the other was teasing her sweet spot more in slow circles. "You're driving me crazy. I missed you so much."

"I missed you too, baby." He bent down and kissed her again as her legs wrapped around him, flipping him onto his back. She didn't think they would stop making love. Each position flowed into the next, and they praised each other. Her arms remained covered in goosebumps and it wasn't from the cool air.

It was love. It was ecstasy.

When he finished, he ordered food because there was no way he would go into the kitchen without bending her over the counter. The pizza was placed by the front door. Casey groaned when he got up from the bed, away from her.

He walked in with the pizza boxes, "The House of Pep for Roni has arrived." Then posed like the statue of library but the pizza boxes were the flames.

"LAME," Casey roared with laughter laying on her side. "Your corniness is too much sometimes but I love it."

"My lady," he said with a now British accent. "The pork covered cheat meal is ready for your excellent pussy having queeness."

When they finished eating, Denver turned on a random movie and they fell asleep holding each other.

The next morning, Casey made a cup of coffee from his

Keurig. She opened the curtains to another breathtaking mountain view. She found the cream and sugar in labeled containers in the designated coffee area. *Okay organized.* When her cup was fixed just how she liked it, she stretched out on his couch and opened her laptop. Then stared at the screen, waiting for something to come to her.

New York was over. The training was over, for now. And the spotlight was back on herself and her goals.

I need to set a launch date. "I am not a punk bitch," she whispered to herself. Casey walked to his calendar and flipped to the month of July. She closed her eyes, held open her pointer finger and landed on a date. July 1st.

She went back to her laptop and opened her business brain dump document, typing in the date. That gave her about two and a half months to promote.

She typed an email to Sky with the launch date and random ideas for gaps in the schedule. Free yoga classes to the public on Sunday afternoons was something she was thinking about for awhile since she practiced it. She was making progress and it made her toes lose feeling. She's always wanted to dance. Routines danced around her head from when she opened her eyes or falling asleep. Owning a studio of her own and teaching other women, especially black woman new skills to make them feel better and healthier, was at the top of her list.

She quickly updated her website and saved it in draft mode, then put the finishing touches to the booking platform. Sky emailed back a thumbs up and a GIF of Kendrick Lamar dancing.

Casey quietly jumped up and danced. *They not like us!* She sat back down and hovered her mouse over the 'publish' button.

Then paused.

What if nobody shows up? What if she falls teaching her

first class and nobody takes her seriously? What if this wasn't what she was meant to do? She glanced at Denver's bedroom door; he was definitely still sound asleep. The sun was only just rising.

She decided to call the only person that would be able to talk her through this, Mama. She answered on the second ring.

"Mama I'm scared. What if I publish the website and do all of this and nobody shows up? There are literally endless bad things that can happen."

"Oh baby." Her mom said sympathetically. "That's always the risk of doing something you love. Even if one person comes, it's a success. If nobody comes, you can promote until you do. But, I think it'll be perfect. You never know what taking this first step may lead you. You've impacted so many lives already across the country. We wouldn't have such a standardized training process if it wasn't for you. You've accomplished so much already with much farther to go. You just have to trust yourself."

Casey's finger hovered over the publish button for her website. "I'm about to publish the website. I think I'm gonna be sick."

"Girl press that button and start your dream! Quit actin scared of it."

Published. "I did it."

"I'm proud of you. You are and will be successful." Hearing Mama say those words brought a wave of calm over her. "One step at a time and you took a big one. I wish I could squeeze you tight. Where are you?"

"I'm in Denver."

"Ohh your in Denver, with the Denver boy I'm assuming."

"Bye Mom gotta go."

Mama roared in laughter. "I love you."

"I love you too Mama." Then they got off the phone.

As the reality was hitting Casey on the website finally being finished, she heard Denver's bedroom door open. "You're awake, baby?"

"Yea, since I'm a couple hours behind time wise, I figured I could get started early doing a little work. Guess what?"

He walked over sleepily and kissed her forehead. "What?"

"I finally published the website."

Joy filled his sleepy face. "Yes! Can I see it? I wanted to give you privacy but tell me the URL right now." Casey texted, passionpolestudios.com to him and he looked through the website. "Case! You did a great job with this layout and pictures."

"Thank you Sky gave a lot of input and suggestions. It definitely wouldn't have looked like this." She said with a chuckle. "You really like it?"

"Yes! So July 1st hmm? I'll need to look at flights because I'll definitely be there. I gotta support you. I love you and I'm always gonna show up for you." He hugged her, tight, like it was one of those hugs where you could take a deep breath.

"Then I can fly out and see you! Mr. Homeowner. I own my condo but damn this is a nice house. Do you film your videos around your house, too?"

He shook his head. "Nope. Just the kitchen and my bed. The world doesn't need to know the layout of this place."

"So your bathtub, there's no videos from there?" He shook his head. "You didn't record anything with your lil bestie Taylor?"

He made a face. "You know jealousy doesn't look cute on you. Also no, I don't record myself with other people. I just like peek shows, masturbation and stuff like that."

She nodded her head. "Okay good because I don't want to see you pounding someone else either. Even if we are 'single'. Any plans for the day?"

"Anything you want to do?"

She eyed his lips then his eyes, "Oh there are a couple of things I want to do."

"You brought the handcuffs, didn't you?"

She smiled, "No not the handcuffs. But I do have my toy collection, in case you get tired."

Denver smiled as he brushed his fingertips on her leg, "Oh you mean my coworkers? We get along fine whether I'm tired or not." She placed her laptop on the end table.

"Let's see about that." She pulled him on top of her as they kissed, his morning wood greeting her.

THEY SAT on the living room floor, watching videos on his TV. "You know I feel bad that I haven't shown you much of the city."

She shrugged. "We had a weeks of buildup to work out of each other. I'm not mad." She lightly shoved him with her foot. "Anything thoughts on dinner?" He quickly grabbed her calf and kissed it. "No no no," she said laughing. "We need real food since we finished the pizza for lunch."

He sighed, "I guess."

She stood up and walked over to the fridge, checking expiration dates and different food. "I'll cook dinner tonight."

His eyebrows raised, "You're cooking for me again? I must really be starting to grow on you."

She threw a plastic fork that hit his head. "Maybe I am! I've already said I love you a few times. Don't make me take it back."

"You couldn't even if you wanted to." He said with a sly smile.

WHEN SHE WAS DONE COOKING dinner, she guided him to the dinner table. He was loving every minute of time they have had together. He knew she wouldn't pack up her home and studio to relocate to him, but he was definitely considering moving to her.

"Sit down," she said with a smile as she placed the plate in front of him.

I've got good dick, she wouldn't kill me now.

"Stop making that face like your scared," she chuckled as she placed a folded piece of paper next to the plate.

His eyebrow arched, "For me?" She nodded. When he opened the paper it said 'Sorry for the wait'. He chuckled as he opened the paper all the way.

Will you be my boyfriend?
Yes or No

HE STARED at the paper then gently touched her handwriting.

"Do you mean it?" He asked. He wasn't going to get hurt again. He still felt humbled from being embarrassed at her birthday party in front of Ayden and everyone else there.

Casey slid a pen across the table, a smile on the corner of her lips. "Check a box and see".

He picked up the pen with a laugh and dramatically checked the "Yes" box and slid the pen and paper across the table.

"It's about damn time." He scooted his chair back and went into his bedroom. When he walked back out, he had a hat in his hand.

"Are we going to a rodeo next?" She asked.

He placed his Stetson on her head and tapped her chin. "I'd love to go to one with you, if your interested. My parents go every year."

She smiled as he quickly picked her up, carefully placing her on the dining table. "This calls for a celebratory dinner and you're the main course."

He tore her panties in two and devoured her. The shock on her face made him plunge his tongue deeper into her. She held onto his hat with one hand, the other was twisted in his hair under her. *Maybe I should've asked him sooner?*

THREE WEEKS LATER, Denver finished a gig at a comedy show in Midtown Atlanta. His contract had been restored after his 30-day suspension. Now that he and Casey were officially dating, it was easier for him to focus on his work again. Bringing the joy to stuffy corporate environments.

When Casey left Colorado, she posted their selfie from Christmas on social media as a post and tagged him, and not the story that disappears in 24 hours. He was surprised at her public expression. He knew she meant what she said about them being official.

When he came back to her condo in Atlanta, Casey was on her laptop sending emails and ordering supplies to prepare for the launch.

He asked, "Is there anything I can do to help with the launch?"

She thought about it. When she came back from New York,

Sky left everything where it was and added shelves. When Casey asked her why, Sky said people needed to have a place to put their things. She was so thankful for her and her forward thinking. "There is something I need help with."

When the arrived to the studio, he looked around nodding his head. "Dang this is actually a good sized space." Then he looked out the window. "Okay walking path view! That's good! People are always walking by right? That's good visibility."

Casey nodded, swinging on one of the poles into a simple spin. "Yea, I'm guessing that's why Mom picked it."

He rubbed his hands together looking at her, "I'm here to help!"

She showed him a video that demonstrated how to make cloud lights. He looked up at the ceiling, "I think this would look great," he told her. When Casey sent the post to the Sky, she agreed that it would look nice and add a cool effect for videos and classes at night. They tapped the poster boards together, superglued the LED lights and added the cotton balls so they looked like real clouds. When it was placed on the ceiling, Casey turned off the lights and turned the clouds on. They looked just as cute as she imagined. Then she turned it to a pink setting.

"Of course," he said with an eye roll.

"Want to learn a move or two?"

"Sure!"

Casey showed him how to grab the pole with his inside arm and walk around. Once he got that, she showed a basic lift and he easily flowed into it. Even spinning a few times.

"Not you having moves!"

He swung his leg around and did a perfect fireman spin while Casey jaw dropped. "So everything just comes easy to you huh."

He hopped off the pole and shrugged. "I may have practiced here and there with my travels."

Casey rolled her eyes. "Thanks for trying to show me off, without even stretching. Do your 'followers' know about this skill?"

"Nope just you," he laughed, then planting a kiss on her cheek.

CHAPTER 26

SINCE CASEY HAD BEEN BACK HOME, she stopped by the studio almost everyday. Checking the poles, testing and checking the security systems, updating the website with class schedules, cleaning and recording promo videos for the launch. She even went live to show some moves with her pointe shoes on. She and Sky also recorded a new duo pole routine they came up with on the spot that got 10,000 views. Even though Casey was nervous, she still kept moving and trying to build more social media attention to her dream. A few people even signed up for the first class on launch day. But Sky said she wasn't allowed to see the list of names.

It was now two days before the wedding, which was also the bachelorette party. Even though Gemini and Calvin only had one best man and maid of honor, Gemini still wanted Casey to be close on the day of. First it was a nail appointment, then to the house rental for the fun part of the night.

She smiled at Gemini widely as they walked into the nail salon. "Hey girl!"

The receptionist smiled widely and came around the desk

to hug Casey. "Hey girl, welcome back! Is this the bridal appointment? Is this the bride?"

Gemini waved her hand and did a half smile. She wore a white crop top with light wash jean shorts and white flip flops. "How could you tell?"

They laughed together. "Congrats anyway! I thought you reserved for 4. Do you want to wait until the other two come?"

Casey looked at Gemini and shrugged. "It doesn't matter to me."

Gemini looked down at her phone, "They just texted and they're about 10 minutes away. We can get started. I have a personal question to ask you anyway."

The receptionist nodded and walked them to the reserved chairs, marked with a sash.

Casey raised her eyebrows. "Ooo I'm all ears."

Sitting down, they both exhaled as the nail techs removed their shoes.

"By the way, I got us all the premium package so hot towel, champagne, the works. All with my new sister," Gemini beamed.

She extended her hand to Gemini and squeezed it tightly. Then as if on queue, two full glasses of champagne were offered to them.

Gemini took a sip and smiled. "Oh it's sweet, I like this. Anyways here's my problem." Casey leaned in and Gemini leaned closer, too. "Which painting in the library is Calvin's? He won't confirm it for me when I ask him."

Casey roared with laughter, wiggling her toes in the warm water. The smell of the essential oils brushed her nose and she immediately relaxed. "I been figured that out girl. You should've been asked."

Gemini rolled her eyes. "How? They all almost look the same. He followed the same theme across the whole library."

"You promise to not tell Calvin?" Gemini nodded in affirmation as her eyes grew wide. "A week after opening, Greg and I went in there and turned over every painting in there. Every fucking one, bitch. He signed it. It's the one with the male character with the glasses and yellow shirt. Greg was cheesing big as fuck when he saw it too. He was happier than me. Then we uh," Casey stuck her tongue out.

The color drained from Gemini's face, "Yall uh what?"

"Girl we fucked, duh. Calvin hated it but." Casey shrugged.

Gemini pressed her lips together hard. "Y- yall fucked?"

Casey did a nervous chuckled. "Gemini, you're stuttering like my brother. What's the problem?"

Gemini stared at her hands, suddenly in awe of the gel machine. Casey stared grinning like a Chester cat. "We're Eskimo sisters! Bitch you could've said something!" Then she lowered her voice to a whisper, "We fucked the same nigga ahh."

Gemini looked at her horrified, "No I couldn't tell you. It was a long night."

Her mouth dropped. "I know you didn't cheat on my brother."

"No no! Uhh he uh."

Casey leaned forward raising her eyebrows, "He uh what. My nails costed too much to mess up. He what?" Then Casey whispered, "He didn't do anything inappropriate, did he?"

"Hell no everything was consensual. But uh Calvin was uh there."

Casey blinked. "We're not talking about this anymore."

Gemini nodded, "Agreed."

There was an awkward silence as the nail techs finished.

"I always knew they liked each other. Welp time to officially take Greg off the roster."

"You have a roster?" Gemini asked.

"Yes duh. Gotta have a lil friend in each city? Why do you think I liked being on the road. But that's not necessary anymore since I'm cuffed."

Gemini shoved her, "You sure are. I saw your 'officially cuffed' post. Yall are so cute. He's coming right?"

"Of course! Denver wouldn't miss it for the world. He's been in town the past couple of weeks since he booked a 6-week gig at a hotel here."

Gemini smiled at her, "I'm so happy for you. I'm glad you stopped being stubborn."

"Me too!"

As the polish was being put on, Aunt Lorraine and Serena walked through the door. They pointed to the receptionist that they were with us and they waved them over. They took seats next to Gemini and gave different updates. Casey was just glad to be close to family folk.

WHEN THEY GOT to the mansion, everyone got comfortable and changed into their matching gold pajama sets. Except for Gemini's hers was white. Even though Aunt Lorraine was invited, she decided not to come. Casey was thankful because even though Aunt Lorraine was cool, she didn't know how cool she would be about what was to come. Serena was preparing margaritas in the kitchen while humming, Gemini was talking to Calvin on the phone and Casey was rolling blunts.

As soon as Gemini got off the phone, Serena collected all of the cell phones and put them in the box.

"Tonight were gonna have fun and have no distractions in celebrating my sis getting MARRIED!"

"Woohoo!" They cheered together.

When Casey imagined weddings, it always had large bridal parties, rows of shots and matching clothes. Gemini and Calvin decided to only have one officially bridesmaid and groomsman. She chose Serena and Calvin chose Greg. Is it weird that Gemini has had sex with the groom and groomsman? Depends on who knows and who asks.

After the blunts were prepared for each lady, Gemini had finished her second glass of wine and she was having fun. When there was a knock at the door Serena gave Casey a devilish grin.

The Surprise.

"Gemini go open the door."

She gave them a speculative stare. "Yall aren't gonna kill me right? If the sister in Bodyguard calls a hit on her sister, yall wouldn't do it to me right?"

They laughed harder, "Girl just open the damn door." Serena said giving her a push towards the door.

Gemini looked through the peephole and her jaw dropped.

The model from the paint and sip, wearing jeans, Timbs and no shirt.

"Are you the gorgeous woman getting married?" He said in a dark deep voice. A voice as deep as his mahogany glistening skin. She turned around and looked at Serena and Casey who waved at him.

"Yes she is." Serena said bringing a chair to the living room floor.

Casey sat Gemini down in the chair and handed her a stack of 100 one dollar bills. "It's my sis last night a fiancé. Can you help her remember it?"

She slowly walked over, rubbing his beard. "I think that can be arranged." Gemini knew this was the model she's been following for awhile; the same one at the paint and sip. He gave her a lap dance that ended with him being naked. Gemini even sneakily licked his dick while they cheered her on. When his hour was up, she was still in a daze.

"How did yall manage to book him and make my dreams come true? Calvin would've lost his mind, in a good way. Whew, where's the blunt?" Gemini said fanning herself. Casey and Serena laughed with her as they lit up. Casey was so glad that she didn't miss this. These were the best times to hang out with the people she loved.

CHAPTER 27

DENVER WAS WAITING for Casey the next day at her place. She caught him up on everything and was still buzzing with fun as they sat on the couch together. She held his hand and looked him in the eye, "Okay so I'm going to ask you question and I want your 100% honest truth opinion okay?"

He placed his other hand on top of hers, "Of course, bae. What's up?"

"How would you feel about me inviting Ayden over and having a little sleepover?"

His eyebrow arched, "A sleepover?" he paused. Casey could feel his mind spinning. She knew Denver and Ayden didn't really get along. Well, more feuded every time they were within three feet of each other. But she had to at least ask.

"I wanted to ask you first because you're most important to me. I know we're still new, but it's something I'm curious about."

She kissed his knuckles. "You make me feel secure in the relationship with the two of us. I just want to explore something, something different with you there."

He half smiled at her as he brushed his thumb across her chin. "I feel more secure with you now too." He kissed her, a meaningful peck. "I'm okay with it. I know it's what you want. I'll let my boundaries known when needed."

She smiled widely. "Yay! Okay I'll call him and see. Since the wedding is tomorrow, he should be in town."

"Mmhm. Let's see if we can be in the same room and not kill each other."

She rolled her eyes as her thumbs moved on her phone screen, hoping Ayden's answer would also be yes.

SHE OPENED the door and Ayden took his shoes off as he walked in. "So this is your place? It looks nice. Is that a Hello Kitty clock in the corner? You just sneak the pink in there don't you."

Casey put on an awkward smile. "Heeey and yes that is. I've had it since I was a kid. Anyways."

Then she saw the moment Ayden's eyes fell on Denver's face. "Oh this nigga."

Denver scoffed loudly. "Didn't you agree to be here?"

"Yea I did. But it just looks like you're not happy to see me, pretty boy."

Denver smiled and rubbed his jaw as he walked up to Ayden. "You know what? I'm not happy. But you should be since, you know, your not in a jail cell right now. Your records public, pretty boy."

Ayden sneered and took a step toward him. "Maybe we do need a lil friendly 60-second fade. If that pressure needs to be met, I got it. Type shit. So what's up?"

Denver grinded his teeth. "Maybe you should've stayed in Casey's past. You barely know the woman she's grown into."

He laughed so loud in response it bounce off the walls. "Who do you think popped her cherry? Punk ass nigga."

Denver lunged at him but stopped himself from throwing the first punch.

Casey stood in between them. "First off, y'all not about to mess up my place. Fuck that."

Denver took a step back to sit on the couch. "I don't have pressure. But I won't turn away from a fight if that's what he wants."

"It ain't that deep." Ayden said sitting at the counter.

She took a deep breath. Maybe this was too big of an ask. "You know what. I'm just gonna roll a blunt and go outside. Y'all are welcome to smoke it with me." She slammed her porch door as she exited and threw herself on the porch chair.

The men looked at each other, then looked away.

"Now I feel like a dick," Ayden mumbled.

"Well you did offer to fight in *my* girlfriend's living room. For what? Because you don't fuck with me." Denver said with crossed arms.

Ayden scoffed. "I wouldn't fuck with you if you were the last man alive."

"I don't fuck with you either." Denver threw. "If we were in the same room and Casey wasn't there, I would be on the wrong block."

There was silence, besides their breathing and brewing hatred. Then Ayden finally spoke, "Look I've disappointed Casey alright? I know I'm just popping back into her life and haven't been positive. I know yall are dating. That's clear. But how about we give her two hours of time without going back and forth."

Denver rubbed his jaw. Ayden and Casey had a history he didn't understand, but had to respect it. "Alright, two hours."

They made eye contact as Ayden walked over, then they shook hands. Now they just had to keep their word.

They both walked to the patio door and knocked, looking at her with apologetic eyes. She frowned, rolled her eyes and waved them out.

"We just wanted to apologize." Ayden started. "We didn't mean to start going back and forth like that in your home. That was disrespectful."

Denver nodded, "Yea we could've been more level headed. We'll act right from now on." She nodded and stood up.

"That's more like it," she said with a low laugh. We can go back inside, it's a little too hot out here."

Once inside, Casey sat next to Denver on the couch, while Ayden sat at the counter.

"So I wanted to talk to you both about something." Their faces twisted. "It's not a threesome I promise." She said deadpan.

The men exhaled loudly, "Thank God." Ayden mumbled. "I wasn't trying to see all that."

"What you think I want to?" Denver chuckled.

"*Anyways*, I just wanted to try something tonight. More like put on a show. You both have been in the same room while I've performed right?"

The men looked at each other then at Casey, "Technically."

She smiled wider. "Perfect, how about I just do a performance and we can see where it goes. Can y'all give me that?"

They nodded.

"Bet. Imma change real quick and come back."

When she returned, it was in a black lace matching bra and thong set. They started breathing harder as her eyes caught each of their attention. Then she got on her hands and knees, giving them a peek of her back door. Megan Thee Stallion was already blasting out of her speaker as she threw her hand behind her shoulder, blowing them kisses. They were locked into her and the moves she made from the bat of her eyelashes to the tip of her blush painted toes.

Her routine was slow. She took her time brushing her hands up her leg, up her chest and across her breast. She winded her hips, placed her hand behind her head and began slowly spinning, building momentum. Then she slowed, coming back to the ground with an effortless turn on her toes. She twerked her way to the floor again, easing into a split.

She stood up on beat and strutted into her bedroom, giving the men the 'come hither' sign with her index finger. Denver and Ayden glanced at each other as they entered the room. She pointed at Denver, then to a small loveseat in the corner. Then pointed at Ayden to sit on the storage cube. The music continued as she crawled onto the bed. Denver began standing up but she raised her hand and lowered it, so he sat back down.

"Just watch me," she whispered. "If you don't want to, feel free to leave."

She laid her head back on her pillows, eyes closed as she brushed her finger tips across her torso, up to the neck, running her fingers through her hair as she took deep breaths. Then she lifted her leg so that her foot was past her head, both her legs extended as she massaged her legs. Her index finger brushed her pearl and she groaned. Then she sucked her finger and returned to the same place.

When she began to plunge, she heard an aching groan from Ayden's corner. She looked at him and met his burning eyes. She inserted a second finger as Denver's green hazel eyes showed through the dark. Her leg twitched, bringing her back to herself.

She quickly sat up, when in her nightstand and turned on her rose.

"Fuck," Denver groaned as the sounds of the vibrations filled the room.

Casey's jaw dropped as her back arched. Then she turned up the frequency, making her toes curl. The sounds of lapping water came as she moaned louder. Then she turned the Rose off and flipped onto her knees so her ass was in their faces.

"Damn Casey," Ayden whispered. "You look good as fuck baby."

Three of her fingers returned inside of her as she began to twist and bounce on her hand. "Yes yes yesss, I'm coming." The sweetness falling onto her hand with a shake. So much pressure released that she just laid down on her side, smiling.

"That is a show I could see anytime," Denver said standing up.

"Hell yea," Ayden said rubbing his chin. "I better go. See yall tomorrow." He gave Denver and Casey a head nod, then left the room then out the front door.

"Well so much for a sleepover," Casey said with a chuckle.

"At least we didn't fight during your performance." Denver said sitting on the bed with her, nudging her with his elbow. She rolled her eyes as she nudged him back. "So can you do that 3-finger bounce on my hand while sitting right above my head?"

She laughed as she began to mount.

CHAPTER 28

AS CASEY WAS UNPACKING HER 'HONORARY' bridesmaid dress, that Gemini shipped for her to try on in New York, Denver was getting dressed in her closet next to her. "So am I going to this wedding as your plus one or your date?"

She looked at him in his emerald honey eyes. "Your coming as my boyfriend. Is that okay with you?"

He smiled and kissed her cheek. "I had to make sure you didn't change you mind after last night."

"I NOW PRONOUNCE you husband and wife! You may kiss the bride," the preacher announced.

Calvin smiled as he lifted the vail over her face. Gemini had tear streaks down her face as she touched Calvin's face. He mouthed something to her that made her laugh, then she grabbed his chin as he grabbed her waist. The crowd cheered as Calvin dipped her, supporting her back.

After they kissed, a loud clap of thunder rang above everyone. It made everyone flinch. Then, the rain started pouring down immediately. As the guests started to stand and cover themselves with jackets and programs. Casey stood up preparing to leave, Denver and Ayden on each side. Denver was holding her hand. Then she glanced at her brother and new sister in law.

They were still staring at each other then back at the alter like the rain wasn't pouring around them, soaking their clothes. Casey stood and watched them. They stared into each other eyes and kissed again, Gemini wrapping her arms around his shoulders. Casey took a couple pictures of them, not caring if her phone died from water damage.

Denver took off his jacket and placed it over Casey's head. "Are you ready to go?"

Casey smiled, knowing that her brother found the one for him. To accept him for him, "Yea."

THE RECEPTION WAS SO much fun! Greg gave a heart felt speech as best man. With Casey now knowing the new developments, she no longer saw Greg as an edible 6-foot chocolate bar. Gemini's best friend Serena sang her speech. Her rich voice resembled Jennifer Hudson. Everyone was either crying or covered in goosebumps.

Calvin and Gemini had their first dance to 'II Hands II Heaven by Beyonce'. The floor around them slowly began to fill with smoke. When the beat slowed down, he wrapped his arm around her back and dipped her again as she laughed. When she was upright, they began to sing word for word with crowd. Casey saw the tears in Calvin eyes as Gemini placed her hand on his chin. She whispered something in his ear that made him lean into her more.

They continued to rock together to the music as the smoke

swirled around them. They looked like they were dancing on a cloud above everyone. Gemini began jumping on beat, then Calvin. Then they motioned everyone to come onto the dance floor. The DJ perfectly transitioned the song and the room erupted. Everyone with drinks in their hand moving across one another. Casey backed up into Denver and danced with him. Ayden was dancing with another girl not too far away. Denver kept up with her tempo with her hand rested at her hip.

After dancing for more than a couple songs, Casey needed a break.

While at the bar, Gemini tapped her on the shoulder and gave her a tight hug. "Thank you for everything and accepting me into your family."

"Girl! Of course. It'll be nice having another girl Grant in the house."

Casey took a deep breath and consumed the energy of the room as Gemini looked at the crowd next to her. "What did Calvin say to you at the alter that made you laugh?"

Gemini chuckled, moving a wet piece of her hair from her forehead. "I can't repeat it, word for word. But in summary, he was glad coming to my car led us here." Gemini laughed harder as Casey looked at her confused. "It's an inside joke Case, but it made me smile."

Casey smiled to herself, "I know you love him. But why did you all get married?"

Gemini glanced at Calvin. He was laughing with Mama as she was fixing his tie. He looked over at her and smiled with his whole face.

"I married Calvin because I couldn't imagine spending another day without him. When we had our little misunderstanding, he made sure to communicate with me moving forward. He's working on himself and always shows me how much he loves me. I'm not perfect either, surprisingly. Whether if it's notes on our fridge, or leaving chocolates on top of the book I'm reading, he always makes it clear where he stands with me. Now that doesn't mean we don't argue, but through it all, he's my number one. Your brother is my soulmate in real life." Then the tears started to fall from both of their eyes.

Casey was glad her brother finally found someone that saw him and allowed him to himself. Maybe she could, too? She looked at Denver and Ayden as they talked at their table. They laughed and dapped each other up. They were finally getting along.

"I'm so happy for you Mrs. Gemini Grant." Casey hugged her again. "GG, I actually love that for you."

"Ahh," Gemini said with a wide grin. "Let's take a shot before I have to be social some more." Suddenly, two tequila shots appeared at the bar. The bartender winked at Gemini as she gave him a cheesy wink. "What should we toast to?"

"To life and the pursuit of happiness." Casey said confidently.

"Here here!"

EPILOGUE

THE JULY SUN was beating down everyone, radiating from the sidewalk. Casey put so much setting spray on her face so that her makeup would be perfect.

Finally, today was the day.

Casey, Sky, Denver and her family stood in front of the studio doors with pink ribbon going across. A small crowd was gathered, some from curiosity and others who signed up for the class happening immediately after.

Casey skipped forward and grabbed the microphone, "Hi everyone! I just want to say thank you for coming out. It has been a journey to get here but we made it! I have a few people that I want to thank. First, my mom the real OG and business owner she built Grant Enterprises and I'm blessed enough to receive an investment from her. I also have to thank my dear friend and business partner, Sky. She kept me together while also holding down the fort when I went out of town."

She reached and squeezed Sky's hand and blew a kiss to Nettie. "Also a shout out to my siblings Calvin and Coraline. Thank yall!" She looked back and waved at them. Calvin awkwardly put his hand up as Coraline had on her CEO smile. "If I thanked everyone that encouraged me, we would be here all day. Are you ready for class?"

"Yes!" the crowd cheered.

Casey waved Sky over as they held the oversized pink handled scissors, cutting the ribbon. When they cut it, Denver stepped to the side and offered to hold the scissors as she turned the key and opened the door.

A new beginning. The beginning she didn't think she would get it.

I'm so glad I didn't delay this anymore, she whispered to herself.

When the crowd disbanded into the studio with 'oos' and 'aahs', she saw more familiar faces.

"Congrats!" Willow-Mae cheered. "We are so proud of you! I know our lil ol' club in New York won't be nothin compared to the talent coming to this studio!" Casey ran and gave her a hug along with the other girls that made the trip to the launch.

The first class was mainly filled with friends, but there were three people she didn't recognize. She still did introductions and made sure everyone knew it was a safe space before starting stretches. While teaching, a joy bubbled in Casey's stomach. She was finally on her own, doing what she loved, while encouraging people to do the same.

When the class concluded, Gemini, Calvin and Coraline stayed behind to help clean up. As Casey was wiping down the poles and Coraline swept, Coraline said "Hey I just want to say I'm proud of you. I really didn't want you to quit the studio in New York, but my hands were tied."

Casey paused and looked at her, "You're leading a big company. I get it. I'm glad I gave you time to find a replacement, like how you threatened."

They laughed lightly, then they hugged.

Calvin snuck a took a picture and they turned to look at him. "I didn't know when that would happen again sorry."

"Grant Family Group hug!" Gemini cheered pulling them all together.

AFTER THREE MONTHS, Casey had secured enough business to be a month ahead on the rent. Not only was she thankful for the support, but a post promoting black owned businesses on the Beltline brought her the most business she had ever seen. Sky and Casey had a full partnership with Sky slowly backing away from her overnight job at the club.

Denver stayed by Casey's side each step of the way. He kept his home in Denver, Colorado, but each visit to Atlanta lasted longer and longer. Would he be able to convince Casey to buying a home with him instead of proposing first?

That dream may need to be deferred.

ACKNOWLEDGMENTS

Oh my gosh! I did it again! Another novel is down and I can't believe it. I wrote the majority of this book while being in postpartum. This book helped keep me grounded when so many changes were happening in my life. I had to find and make time for myself, while fighting for my dream. Casey helped me fall back in love with writing while giving me the hope I needed to keep going.

I would like to first thank God for allowing these words to come to me and for this book to see the light of day. I would also like to thank my husband, Antonio, and our blessing of a daughter. Thank you for your patience while I was typing my life away. My muffins mean the world to me and have helped this novel come to be.

I would also like to thank Che'Naomi Durant (IG @withloveOG) for doing this beautiful book cover and Chelsia McCoy (IG @coach_chelsiamccoy) for doing an amazing job amplifying the characters voices by editing this work. I truly enjoyed working with a team of black women to bring Casey Grant's story to life.

Thank you to my community of friends and family for keeping me encouraged and supporting my dreams.

I also want to encourage you, the reader, to do something nice for someone else. You never know what people are going through and something small to you, could be big for them.